K. ELLIOTT

Published by Urban Lifestyle Press
P.O. Box 12714
Charlotte, NC 28220

www.ulppublishing.com

Editor: Inkeditor Staff

Cover Design: www.mariondesigns.com

Book Layout: Shawna A. Grundy
                       ShaGru Entertainment
                       www.shawnagrundy.com

First printing January 2006

10 9 8 7 6 5 4 3 2 1

ISBN: 09717697-2-9

Acknowledgements

I would like to thank God. Without God nothing is possible. My parents Otis and Margaret Douglas, Sharon Fincher, thank you for everything, my assistant Sumayah, Ron and Jackie Hargette, Melvin and Shana Wilson; (Melvin you are the best friend a guy could have, very loyal and supportive; they don't get no better than you). Nakea Murray; the best book publicist in the business, here's another bestseller, we are going to the top baby! Toni Green and Pricilla from Pretty Special Inc. Les Bird; thanks for your proofing and input, Rakeeda Leaks thanks for your proofing, James B. Sims of the Inkeditor Staff, thanks for the editing. Author Thomas Long, you are the man; keep holding it down in B-Moore. La Jill Hunt; do your thang Drama Queen. Danielle Santiago; my homie, keep getting down for yours; we'll meet at the top. Tushonda Whitaker, you have a bright future. I just wish I had half your work ethic; you're a true talent. Hallema, what can I say about you? ... I don't know where to begin. I'm glad to have a friend like you. Over the last couple of years we have grown to have a brother-sister relationship. I am blessed to have a friend like you to tell me when I'm wrong because you know that no one can tell K. Elliott anything. But for real; thanks for being down for your boy. Jamise Dames, Treasure Blue, Nikki Turner, K'wan, Shannon Holmes, Mark Anthony Eric Gray, Anna J, Shawna Grundy, Autumn Knight, S.W. Smith, Brandon McCalla, and every other author that I've met along the way. Peace out.

PROLOGUE

J-Black was the neighborhood stickup kid. Jason Black had started his robbing career at the age of nineteen. He had held up seventeen convenient stores but had been convicted of only two of them. He'd served a mandatory eight years before being released at the age of twenty-six. After getting out of prison, he decided that convenient stores wasn't the way to go. Drug dealers were. They were easy prey, and they weren't likely to go to the police for fear of being exposed.

J-Black was a small guy. He was about five nine in height and chiseled from his penitentiary stay. He had a long scar on his neck from a stabbing that had happened in the pen during a fight.

He and Twin met at Burger King to discuss the plans for a robbery over Whoppers and fries. "So who the fuck is this nigga?" J-Black asked.

"Fatboy, and he live on the lake."

"What lake?"

"Norman ... Lake Norman."

"So the nigga got serious paper, huh?" J-Black said as he put ketchup on his fries. He licked a dab that had gotten on his greasy fingers.

"Yeah, the nigga got it like that. I mean, he's getting bricks. You know what I mean?"

J-Black squinted his eyes. "So what the fuck do you want out of the deal?"

"I just want you to split everything with me for putting you up on the lick."

J-Black looked at Twin's Rolex—white gold with a diamond bezel. "Don't look like you doing too bad yourself."

"I'm doing okay."

"Can I see that watch?"

Twin thought about it for a moment.

"Nigga, why you hesitating? Let me see the watch."

"I'm not hesitating; I'm just thinking." Twin sipped his drink then took a bite of his Whopper. Then he took the watch off and passed it to J-Black.

"This is a real nice watch. Let me wear it; I'll give it back in a couple of weeks."

"No. Give me my watch back." Twin said as he reached for the watch.

But J-Black had put the watch on his wrist. "Nigga, you gonna trip about a petty- ass watch and I'm about to get this nigga for bricks."

"Naw, I ain't tripping. Just make sure I get half."

"Okay, the nigga lives on the lake. Where?"

"The Peninsula."

"The Peninsula? How the fuck did he get his ass up there and those crackers ain't called the police on his dope-dealing ass yet?"

Twin shrugged. "I don't know, but the best way to get him is to follow him home."

"From where?"

"My house. I'm supposed to meet him in the morning. When he's on his way, I'll let you know."

J-Black finished his Whopper in two bites. He left wearing Twin's watch.

CHAPTER 1

Tommy found solitude at the lake. Fishing had been one of his favorite hobbies since he was a kid. It was one of those things that he used to like doing with his mama. She was a country girl who loved to fish and cook. She first took him to the lake, where she'd given him his first fishing pole, at the age of seven. At the age of eight he had gotten his first fishing reel. Back in those days, they would come out to the lake and fish for meals. Now, Tommy liked fishing for the peace of mind he got every time he came to the lake. This is where he would reflect upon his life.

Today, when he arrived at the lake, he was still thinking about Nia and what she'd said about his mother being dead. It took every ounce of his self-control to keep from punching her in the mouth. He thought about his mother's complications with breast cancer. She was only forty-eight when she passed a couple of years ago.

He'd chosen to stand on the bank today rather than get in his boat. He had been standing on the bank for ten minutes before he got a bite—a largemouth bass. He heard the sounds of a car stereo coming from over the hills. Rap music.

A few minutes later his friend Twin appeared. "Fatboy, I say what's up nigga. Figured you were down here."

Fatboy had been his nickname since he was in the first grade. It had been given to him by his mama's boyfriend, J.C., the only father Tommy had ever known. Six years ago, J.C. was given ten years for rape. Tommy still visited and sent him money once a month.

Tommy turned and smiled. "What's up, Twin?"

"Not much. Had to get out of the house before I fucked Nia up."

"I know what you mean. I want to fuck my girl up a lot of times."

"Don't they make you mad?"

Twin lit a cigarette. "Hell yeah."

"How do you keep from fucking your girl up?"

"I just get the hell out of the house like you did."

Tommy felt more tugging on his reel. His stopper sank, indicating that there was something on his line. Another bass. Tommy struggled a little before pulling the bass out of the water.

"Damn, nigga. That's a pretty big one."

Tommy took the fish off the hook and tossed it in the bucket.

"Why do you still come down here? I mean, you have so much money now. Why not go buy fresh fish to eat."

"I do this for fun—a stress reliever. I don't even eat fish no more. Don't you still have something that you like to do from when you were a kid?"

"Not really," Twin said. "All I want to do is keep making this dough."

"I know what you mean. I'm just about ready to go back to Miami to get more product."

"What's the problem?"

"We don't have anybody to bring it back to Charlotte."

"That can't be the only problem."

"Yes, it is."

Twin blew out a ring of smoke then squinted his eyes.

Tommy knew that look. He had seen it ever since he was six years old. "So what do you have in mind?"

"I know a couple of bitches that wouldn't mind making some extra money."

"How we gonna get it back, nigga? I mean, security is too tight. On the news, some cats from Colombia were trying to bring it in through the airport. And here is the funny part about it: They had it in their stomachs. They were caught by customs, taken to the hospital, and had their stomachs pumped. Then they were arrested."

"Yeah, somebody told on them."

"You are a fucking genius, Twin."

"You don't get it, do you, nigga? Those cats were probably low on the totem pole, and somebody gave them up so the big package could get through."

"Yeah, right. You've been watching too much television."

"But don't worry about transporting the dope back—'cause I'll be responsible for that."

"We are talking about twenty kilo's, nigga. This ain't no small-time."

"Nigga, just trust me. I can get it back."

"How you gonna do that?"

Twin's eyes squinted again. "I told you I got some broads that are in desperate need of money."

"So let's leave in the morning."

"Let's do it."

*****

Tommy, JoJo, Twin, and Jennifer stepped off the plane in Miami at 10:15 a.m. Tommy rented an SUV. They drove it to South Beach and checked into the South Seas Hotel.

Two hours later the girls arrived. Nicole and Sandy were very attractive. Twin introduced them to JoJo and Tommy.

"So... we gonna have some fun or what?" Twin said with his girlfriend Jennifer clinging to his arm. She was whiter than most Caucasians—blonde hair, blue eyes, perfect white teeth, and a physically fit body. It was important for her to be in shape; she was a stripper at the Uptown Carousel.

"I want to go to the club. All the rappers be hanging out down here," Nicole said.

"What club is that?" Twin asked.

"Club Z-No."

"We can do that, but first we need to go shopping to make sure everybody is looking like a million bucks,—'cause tonight the sky is the limit. We're going to VIP, and we're going to drink champagne and just celebrate life. We're young and we are going to have fun tonight." Twin smacked Jennifer's ass.

Nicole rubbed JoJo's hairy chest. Sandy smiled at Tommy.

At the mall, the girls went on a mini shopping spree. Tommy had gotten upset because he felt they were spending too much money on the girls.

Twin pulled him aside. "Listen, nigga. We gotta get these bitches whatever they want."

"What are you talking about?"

"They're going to make sure the twenty kilos get back."

"I still don't understand," Tommy said.

Twin patted him on the back. "Don't worry about it. Just relax and let me handle this."

*****

Club Z-No was crowded. People were nearly standing on top of each other. The three couples sat in VIP and ordered three bottles of champagne.

JoJo and Nicole were getting acquainted. "So where do you live?" he asked.

"In Charlotte. Just moved here from Ohio." She smiled.

"You know, I'm really feeling you?"

She giggled a little. "No, I didn't know that."

He took her hands. "Damn. You are so soft."

"Am I supposed to be hard?"

"Hell no. If you were I wouldn't be here with you."

"You're funny."

"So, am I gonna get to see you when we get back to Charlotte?" he asked.

"That's up to you."

Twin interrupted by pulling JoJo aside. "Don't try to get next to these broads, man."

"Why not?"

"'Cause you don't want them to know anything about you, just in case anything happens to them. You know what I mean?"

"I hadn't really thought about that, but I guess you're right."

JoJo rejoined Nicole on the sofa but avoided personal questions.

*****

Tommy met Manny the Cuban, at the Mynt lounge on South Beach.

"My friend," Manny said as he gave Tommy a hug. They took seats at the bar. Manny ordered two vodka and cranberry juices.

"I need about twenty kilos."

"Don't have it ... but I can get you ten."

"I'll take it."

"So, are you still fuckin around with that Twin guy?"

"Yeah," Tommy said. He knew that Manny didn't care for Twin too much, even after meeting only once to do business. Twin's money was extremely short, and that didn't set right with Manny.

"I don't know... there is something about that guy that just ain't right."

10

"Ever since we were kids, people in the neighborhood called him the evil twin but—"

"And you still dealing with him?" Manny took a big gulp of his drink and said "I just don't want anything to happen to you."

Tommy didn't respond; he just stared at him. Manny was in his early forties, and he was in great shape because of his morning jogs. His hair wasn't graying; and his tan skin had no wrinkles. He'd lived a great life, one of wealth and prosperity.

"Another round of drinks," Manny said to the bartender.

Twenty minutes later, they were on their way to Manny's mansion, a place where the two of them could comfortably handle the transaction.

CHAPTER 2

DEA agent Mark Pratt had received a call from an anonymous caller. He and his partner, Ken Clarkson, drove to the airport and met with security.

When the plane arrived, it was easy to spot the women. They were the only two African-American women on the plane. Security approached them first.

"What the hell is going on?" one of the ladies asked.

"I need you two to come with me."

"Where are we going?" the same lady asked.

"I just need to ask you a few questions." The man pointed to an office behind him.

The ladies were hesitant.

Mark Pratt walked over and flashed his badge. "I'm Mark Pratt of the DEA; and this is my partner Ken Clarkson."

Tears rolled down Sandy's face. She looked helplessly at Nicole.

*****

"I think the girls got busted," Twin said as he paced in Fatboy's den.

Fatboy picked up the remote control then muted the television." Why do you say that?"

"Every time I call the phone, it goes straight to voice mail."

"Really?" JoJo asked.

"Yeah, but we can't let that worry us. Paige made it through safely, so we got plenty of dope."

"We should be worried. Those girls know how all of us look. That's the same way Jamal and Dawg went down—a couple of bitches brought everybody down."

"Jamal went out in a blaze of Glory." Fatboy smiled. "Yeah, that nigga was the realest nigga to ever come out of my hood."

Jamal had been a couple of years older than him, but they were from the same neighborhood and used to get their haircut at the same barbershop. Fatboy remembered all the cars and the beautiful women Jamal had had.

"I ain't trying to go out like that," JoJo said. "I heard the same agent named Pratt stayed on their ass. I still remember the name."

"Jamal and Dawg were stupid, man. They had too many people in their business, and Dawg had partnered up with the undercover and didn't even know it," Twin said.

"I guess we're too smart and we can never go to jail. It can never happen to us, right?" Fatboy said.

"I know it can't happen to me; because I ain't selling shit to nobody I don't know."

Fatboy grimaced. "You know what, Twin? My dad told me that if I'm ever around a muthafucka who don't think he can go to jail, get the hell away from him."

Twin lit a cigarette. "Hey, I didn't say we can't go, but I know we are smarter than Jamal and Dawg."

"Yeah, but we have to learn from their mistakes. We have get out when it gets hot or else," Fatboy said.

"You know what? Dawg was stupid for selling to the feds; and I don't feel sorry for Jamal—cause the nigga had HIV and was still running around here poisoning chicks with his dirty dick. He gave shorty that shit and ruined her for life."

"Fuck all that history talk; we have eight kilos. Let's get down to business," Twin said, then he blew a ring of smoke around the room.

"How in the hell did Paige make it?" JoJo said.

"She wanted to go by herself," Twin said. "Plus she's white. This is her country, man. Ain't nobody gonna fuck with a white girl."

"Okay...where's our shit?"

"I'll go get it. It's in the car."

*****

JoJo slapped Nia's ass hard as he entered her from the back. The tattoo of the Tiger on her back made his erection harder. He thrusted deeper before turning her over on her side.

"Yes. I love it!" she screamed.

He smiled and kept humping.

Five minutes later, she turned toward him. He examined her body. No stretch marks or cellulite or anything.

She kneeled and put her lips on his manhood. He grabbed her head. She stopped. "You know I don't like it when you do that shit."

He frowned. "Come on, baby, keep going."

Nia wiped her mouth. "You know I can't have you degrading me."

"Is that what this is all about? Degrading? I thought we were just fucking and having fun."

"Yeah, we are, but you know I got a man."

"The one I've known all my life."

"And I feel bad about doing this shit sometimes."

"Hell, me too."

"I can't tell; you grabbing my head and shit, trying to make me feel like some slut toy."

JoJo stood and picked his boxers up from the floor. "You're the one that started this shit."

Nia picked up a Timberland boot and threw it at JoJo. "Motherfucker, you gonna put this shit all on me? Remember, you're the one that used to come around while Fatboy was gone and tell me how nice my ass was."

"But you're the one that used to wear all that revealing shit around the house. You wanted me to look at your ass."

"Fuck you, JoJo."

He walked over, grabbed Nia by the arm, and kissed her forehead. "I'm sorry. We like each other. That's all that matters."

She leaned forward and kissed him. "I love Fatboy, too."

"I know you do."

"I'm in a fucked up situation."

"Think about me; I'm the nigga's friend from day one."

"What are we gonna do?"

"I don't know."

Nia's eyes became moist. She stepped away from JoJo's grip then turned to face him. "I keep telling myself that Fatboy's impotence is the reason I'm cheating."

"Well it is, isn't it?"

"That and the fact that I like you ... I like the way you make me feel, and I like the way you make me laugh."

"I like you, too, Nia."

"Come and give me a kiss, nigga."
JoJo walked over to Nia.
She pulled his penis out and continued her oral performance.

CHAPTER 3

Her name was Paige Howard, but her stage name was Jennifer. She was a bleached blonde with blue eyes and 38 DD breast implants. Her ass was well-defined from working out at the gym.

It was Tuesday night when DEA agents Mark Pratt and Ken Clarkson strolled into the club. Jennifer was on the stage with a slew of mesmerized men around her, all wanting a part of the woman with the big hooters and the veneered smile.

"I love you," said an older white man wearing a John Deere ball cap.

Jennifer blew him a kiss then motioned for him to come to her.

He walked over right away, his eyes on the double D's. He stepped on stage with two twenty-dollar bills in his hand.

Jennifer grabbed the money and gave the man a kiss, leaving traces of orange lipstick on his jaw. He grinned. She took his ball cap, rubbed it between her legs, and placed it back on his head.

He took the cap off his head and licked it, giving himself some sort of satisfaction. "I love you, Jennifer," he said, smiling.

She stepped back and pulled her G-string to the side, revealing her vagina for a brief second. The crowd tossed a flurry of fives and tens to the stage.

When she was finished, she picked up her money and strutted off stage, disappearing.

A redhead came over smiling at Mark and Ken. "How bout a dance, guys?"

"Who was the blonde?" Mark asked.

"Jennifer. Do you want me to get her?"

Mark pulled out two dollars and passed them to the redhead. "If you don't mind."

She looked at the money, frowned, then passed it back. "Keep your money, hun. I mean, if this is all you got, don't even worry about it."

Mark took the money, folded it, and put it in his wallet.

Minutes later, Jennifer came over to their booth with a white skirt and garter. She looked at Mark. "Hey, good looking." Then she turned to Ken. "Hi, sexy."

Mark extended his hand. "I'm Chris, and this is my friend Dave."

"So you guys want some entertainment or some company?"

Mark and Ken looked at one another.

"Come on, guys. I hope you aren't wasting my time," Jennifer said. She then folded some bills and put them in her garter belt.

"Actually, I wanted to talk to you for a minute."

"Well, can you at least buy me a drink?"

"Mark looked at the money in her garter belt. There had to be at least three hundred dollars, he figured. And she was asking him to buy her a drink.

"I'll buy the drink. What'll you have?" Ken asked.

"Vodka and tonic." Jennifer sat on Mark's lap. "I want a double."

The waitress came and Ken ordered Jennifer's drink along with two bottled waters."

"What are you two guys, cops or something?" Jennifer put her hand on Mark's dick.

He pushed it away. "Why do you ask that?"

"A clean-cut black guy and a clean-cut white guy together in a strip club, ordering waters to drink."

"You think we're cops, huh?" Mark said.

Jennifer reached for Mark's dick again, but again he moved her hand away. "You see, that's what I mean."

"What are you talking about?" Ken asked.

"Cops are the only guys that would move a woman's hand away from his dick."

The waitress came with the drinks. Ken gave her a twenty and she disappeared.

"So what if I told you I am a cop?" Mark said.

"I haven't done anything wrong," Jennifer said, then stirred her drink and took a sip.

"You're not supposed to drink at work."

"You are a cop, aren't you?"

"I am," Mark answered.

Jennifer's eyes grew big. "Am I going to jail?"

"Depends," Ken said. He took a drink of his water.

"Depends on what?"

"Depends on if you are willing to help us."

"Help you do what?"

Mark pulled out his badge. "I'm with the Drug Enforcement Agency."

"What the hell do you want with me?"

"Do you know a guy called Twin?"

"No, I don't know nobody by that name."

"I think you do. We know you were in Miami the other day with him," Ken said.

Jennifer sipped her drink without responding.

"Weren't you in Miami a couple of days ago?"

"Maybe ... maybe not. You're the feds, you tell me." Jennifer hopped off Mark's lap and was about to walk away.

"Paige Howard," Mark yelled out.

Jennifer turned. "How did you know my name, nobody calls me Paige."

"Telephone bill. Your cell phone is in your name. Your number is 777-9301."

"How did you get my number?"

"We're the feds. Remember." Ken said, smiling.

Jennifer sat beside Mark again. "What do you want with me?"

"We want you to tell us about Twin."

"I don't know anybody by that name."

The redhead came back to the table. She sat beside Ken and smiled.

"Hi," he said.

"Do you need some company?"

"Actually, I don't have any money."

The redhead stood and said, "What the hell are you in a strip club for?"

"Entertainment, honey." He pulled the back of her skirt up, revealing her ass.

"You loser." The redhead swiped at his hand then walked away.

"Okay, Paige, you were in Miami, right?" Mark asked.

"You already know that."

"And you called me and told me that two girls were coming through the airport carrying drugs."

"I didn't."

"Somebody did from your phone. I have a copy of your record, remember?"

"What do you want from me?"

"I want you to be honest with me."

"And if I don't?"

"You can find yourself in big trouble," Ken said.

"I don't like him," Jennifer said to Mark.

"A pretty little girl like you wouldn't survive a day in prison," Mark said.

"Martha Stewart survived, and I'm a lot tougher than her."

"Yeah, Martha had four months. Drug trafficking, the last time I checked, carried a mandatory minimum of ten years. Do you think you can do ten years, honey?" Mark inquired.

"I'm not a drug trafficker."

"That's not what I heard."

"Okay, Jennifer, do you want to help us or not?" Ken added.

"I think she wants to play hardball and do twenty years."

"Twenty years for what? I helped you, remember? I'm the one that called you and told you about the girls coming through the airport."

"So it was you after all." Mark smiled.

"I need another drink."

Mark flagged the waitress and had another vodka and tonic delivered to the table.

Jennifer stirred her drink with the tiny red straw. A pop song played in the background. "So what do you want to know?"

"I want to know about Twin."

"That's my boyfriend."

"Okay...and what else?"

"I don't know what to tell you."

"The girls that got busted told us that Twin was the one that put them up to trafficking the drugs."

"Why would you believe some criminals?"

"They weren't criminals until Twin put them up to bringing the dope back from Miami," Ken said.

"You got it all figured out, huh, white boy?" Jennifer said.

"You didn't look like you had a whole lot of rhythm up there on stage yourself."

Jennifer stuck her tongue out and gave him the middle finger.

"You're not in trouble," Mark said.

"Good,—cause I was about to call my lawyer."

"You don't need a lawyer yet," Ken said.

"Yet? What the hell is he talking about?"

"We know Twin is a drug trafficker, and we know that he put those girls up to bringing that dope back."

"Why don't you go arrest him?"

"Because we know you had something to do with it. You were on the same flight as the girls, and you called from your cell phone to tell us that the girls were bringing drugs through."

"Okay."

"Why would you do that?"

Jennifer stirred her drink, removed the straw from the glass, and licked it slowly. Mark was slightly aroused. "Why would you do that?"

"I did it out of concern."

Ken narrowed his eyes. "Were you really concerned, or did you want to divert the attention away from you?"

"Attention from me? What the hell do you mean?"

"I don't know," Mark said, then sipped his water. "I'm going to take a shot in the dark. Maybe you were carrying product yourself. It's done every day."

"Yeah, right." Jennifer stood, walked off, and looked back at the agents. "I have no time for this bullshit."

"Okay, Paige, you can talk to us now or talk to us later, but rest assured you will talk to us."

"I don't think so. Have a good night, gentlemen."

*****

It was three in the morning when Jennifer got dressed. She unfolded all of her money. The total was $517. Not bad for a Tuesday night. Tuesdays were usually slow and she averaged somewhere between two and three hundred dollars, so she was not complaining about tonight. There was nobody else in the locker room, and she knew she had to hurry if she wanted the bouncers to escort her to her car.

Five minutes later, Bobo the bouncer knocked on the door. "Come on, Jennifer, I gotta go home to wifey. Hurry up."

"Bobo, hold on a second, sweetie. I just got to brush my hair."

"Come on, Jennifer. It's three in the morning. Nobody gives a fuck about your hair."

"Bobo, I'm going to take care of you," Jennifer said. She would give Bobo a twenty for being patient with her.

He was used to her being the last one, and he would wait on her because he knew she would tip him generously, something the other strippers didn't do.

Finally Bobo opened the door and said, "Jennifer, I'm gone. I have to take my little girl to school in three hours. I need to get at least two hours of sleep."

Jennifer stuffed all of her costumes into a designer overnight bag and followed Bobo out.

She fired up the black CLK, pulled out of the parking lot, then hit the interstate. She was bobbing her head to Lil John and the Eastside Boyz when she noticed a state trooper behind her. She switched lanes.

The trooper followed suit. She reduced her speed from sixty-five mph to fifty-five mph.

Moments later the trooper flashed his blue lights.

She pulled to the side of the road.

The tall, slender state trooper asked for her license and Registration.

Jennifer fumbled a bit in her glove compartment then asked, "Sir ,what did you pull me over for?"

"You were speeding more than ten miles over the speed limit, and you swerved."

"Okay." Jennifer smiled. "Can't you just give me a warning?"

He covered his nose. "What in the world have you been drinking?"

"I had a couple of drinks, but I'm not drunk."

"Where is your license and registration?"

"I can't find the registration."

"Out of the car, ma'am."

Jennifer grabbed her sweater from the backseat then got out of the car.

"Okay, ma'am, walk this straight line," the trooper said, pointing to the line on the shoulder of the highway.

Jennifer attempted to walk the line but stumbled slightly.

"Ma'am, I want you to take a breathalyzer."

"I will do no such thing."

"Are you refusing?" the trooper asked. He looked directly into Jennifer's eyes.

"I ain't drunk."

A black Chevrolet SUV drove up. Agents Clarkson and Pratt jumped out of the vehicle. "Jennifer! How ya doing?"

"Heckle and Jeckle ... I know you two had something to do with this shit."

"And you are so fuckin funny. You must be Ellen DeGeneres," Ken said.

"No, just trying to keep from cursing somebody's ass out."

"Trooper, did you search her car?" Mark asked.

"No, not yet."

"I'm not consenting to a search or a breathalyzer."

"You see, Jennifer, you really don't have a choice in the matter now."

"You motherfuckers! You had the trooper pull me over."

"Prove it."

"Trooper, can I borrow your flashlight for a minute?" Ken asked.

The trooper handed him the flashlight.

Ken opened all of the doors of Jennifer's Benz. He searched the back seats and then the front seat. He pulled a half-smoked blunt from the ashtray, showed it to Jennifer, and smiled.

"That's only a hundred dollar fine," she said.

"Oh, yeah. I know you got plenty of money; you're a showgirl." He laughed.

"That's right, cornball. I'm a showgirl, just like your mama was."

He grabbed Jennifer's purse from the front seat of the car. Two yellow pills with an X on each of them fell out of the purse.

"Jennifer, what are these?"

"Those are for my sinuses."

Ken showed them to Mark. "Looks like X to me."

"I don't give a damn what they look like. They are for my sinuses."

"We'll have them tested, and if this is ecstasy ... I will make sure you get indicted. You know what you can get for possession of X?" Ken asked.

"Five years per pill," Mark lied.

Jennifer covered her face and began to cry.

Mark put his arms around her shoulder. "Jennifer, do you want to help us now? I want to help you. I don't want to send you to jail. You don't deserve that."

Jennifer looked up at Mark. "What do you want me to do?"

"We just want you to tell us the truth."

"What do you want to know?"

Mark pulled a card from his wallet then handed it to Jennifer. "Come to my office tomorrow and we will forget all about the ecstasy. If you don't, I will have to charge you."

"What is the best time?"

"Two p.m."

Jennifer wiped her eyes with her hands. "Thank you for not taking me to jail."

The trooper wrote her a warning ticket. He ordered her to leave the car because he would take her home.

CHAPTER 4

Fatboy had just dropped two kilos off at Twin's house. J-Black tailed him in a white work van; two to three car lengths behind him.

Fatboy stopped at a gas station, and J-Black parked at the Waffle House across the street. Ten minutes later, Fatboy stopped and got a pedicure.

J-Black waited in another parking lot, reading the sports section of the *USA Today*. "Bitch-ass nigga."

Finally, after Fatboy had run all his errands, he drove home.

"Damn, this muthafucka got it going the fuck on," J-Black said to himself. He got out of the work van, which had *Lakewood Home Improvement* on the side panels. He walked to the house and rang the bell.

Fatboy came to the door drinking bottled water.

"Damn, you live here, bro?" He stood in wrinkled overalls.

"Yeah."

J-Black smiled. "I love to see us brothers doing good."

"Yeah, I know what you mean? But what can I do for you?"

"Actually, I have my own home improvement service, and I was just wondering is there anything that you would like to improve on your home, though I couldn't imagine what. Man, this thing is amazing. How many square feet do you have here?"

"Forty-five hundred."

"Man, my whole family could live in here."

"So what's your name?"

"Kenny. Kenny White."

"Kenny, I'm Tommy. So what kind of home improvement do you do?"

"Floors ... you know ... painting, cabinets ... you name it. I can do just about anything."

"You do hardwood flooring?"

"I'm the best." J-Black smiled. He'd never even polished a floor.

"Okay, I was thinking of putting some hardwood floors down. How much do you charge?"

"First I would have to measure your floors."

"Cool."

"A'ight. I'll go get the tape measure from the van. I'll be right back."

In the back of the van, he retrieved a sawed-off pump shotgun and eased it down the leg of his pants, concealing it.

Fatboy's door was still open. J-Black walked in and found him with his back turned, feeding fish in a huge in-wall aquarium. J-Black pulled the pump out and put it against Fatboy's back. "Nigga, I will blow a hole in your back. Where is the goddamn money?"

Fatboy raised his arms.

"Put your arms down. I ain't tell you to do shit."

"What did I do to you, man?"

"Don't say shit. Just sit on that chair over there by the fireplace."

Fatboy complied.

"You see, nigga, you ain't gotta do nothing wrong. It's just the fact that niggas is hungry out here. You got it and I want it."

"What do you want? Some money?"

J-Black stared at Fatboy. He could see the tears welling up in the man's eyes. He'd seen that look so many times. He loved to see people in fear. "Damn right I want money. I want money, and I want dope. Where is the dope?"

"What are you talking about? I don't sell dope."

"You think I'm stupid? I know you ain't got this mini mansion legitimately. Where is the muthafuckin dope?"

"I ain't got no dope."

J-Black walked over to the trembling man then placed the gun up to his temple. "You ain't got no fuckin head if you keep lying. Now do you want to tell me where the fuckin dope is, or do you want me to scatter your brains out over this room?"

"In the kitchen ... The dope is in the kitchen."

"Take me to the kitchen."

In the kitchen, Fatboy reached underneath the sink and pulled out six kilos of coke and gave it to J-Black.

"Now this is more like it. Where is the money?"

"Upstairs."

"Lead the way."

Upstairs, Fatboy opened a small *Sentry* safe, located in the closet of his master bedroom, and dumped the money on the bed. "Twenty thousand dollars."

"Nigga, is this all your bitch ass got?"

"Y-yeah, man, this is all I have."

"I see your life don't mean shit to you." J-Black squinted his eyes.

"What do you mean?"

"I'mma kill your bitch ass unless you come up with some more dough."

"Listen, man, I got jewels and watches and shit."

"I want that and I want at least twenty thousand more dollars, or I'll blow your fuckin brains out."

Fatboy pulled opened a dresser and removed a jewelry box. "Here is a watch that's worth forty thousand dollars. It's my girl's."

J-Black snatched the watch then slapped him across the forehead with the butt of the gun. "Now lay the fuck down and close your eyes. If you open your eyes, I'm blasting on your punk ass. You understand me?"

"Yeah."

*****

When J-Black pulled into a *Taco Bell* parking lot, Twin was sitting behind the wheel of a blue Benz. J-Black grabbed the bricks from underneath the seat then jumped in the car with Twin.

"So what you looking like?" Twin asked.

"What the fuck is that supposed to mean? The nigga only had six bricks. You was talking like he was Noriega or somebody. I've had bigger licks than this."

"So where is my three?"

J-Black squinted his eyes. "Nigga, it ain't even going down like that. I'm giving you one brick. That's all you getting."

"That wasn't the deal."

"I don't give a fuck about no deal. Do you know the nigga saw my face? I'm the one at risk, so I don't give a fuck about no deal, you understand?"

"Black ... that shit ain't right, man."

"Life ain't right; you either take it or leave it."

"Give it here. I'll just know the next time that you ain't gonna play fair."

J-Black handed him the brick. "You just better hope I don't ever get the notion to rob your bitch ass," he said, then hopped out of the Benz, got into his work van, and drove off.

*****

Twin's phone rang and he picked it up on the first ring. The caller ID displayed *Tommy Dupree*. "Yeah what's up, Fatboy?"

"I've been robbed, man."

"You bullshittin," Twin said.

"No, I'm not man. I'm serious. Some nigga came over here dressed like a home improvement guy and robbed me at gunpoint, and JoJo is over here now."

"So what did he take from you?"

"He took product ... He took product and jewels and money."

"Yeah?"

"Yeah, man. I remember the nigga's face. I'm gonna send a team after him."

Twin began feeling uneasy. "Hey, listen, I have to go. I have to go see Jennifer's family about something."

*****

"Twin is acting all nonchalant, like he don't give a fuck that I've been robbed."

"He probably don't give a fuck, as long as it wasn't him," JoJo said.

"If it had been him who got robbed, I would be at his house trying to find the muthafucka who did it."

JoJo walked to the kitchen, grabbed a cranberry juice, then said, "See, that's what your problem is. You always think he gives a fuck about you. Listen, man, just 'cause you would do something for somebody don't mean they would do the same for you, you know? Twin has been a grimy-ass nigga since we were kids."

Nia entered the kitchen. "JoJo, I've been telling his ass this since day one, but he seems to think that people care about him. Twin ain't your friend."

"He damn sure ain't."

28

Fatboy made eye contact with Nia. "Would you let me and JoJo have some privacy, and stay in a woman's place."

Nia folded her arms. "That's why you got robbed, nigga."

"Fuck you! Get out of here."

Nia burst through the double doors that led to the living room.

"Back to what I was saying. Twin grew up with us, but he ain't your friend."

Fatboy glanced at JoJo. "I just get a funny feeling about this whole incident."

"What do you mean?"

"I don't know ... Maybe like somebody told this guy who I was and where to find me."

"You think it was Twin?"

"Naw, I don't think Twin would do something like that. I really don't."

*****

Jennifer was a little uneasy about going to the DEA's office to meet with Agent Pratt, but she didn't want to be charged with possession of ecstasy. She'd remembered one of her customers, Gino the Italian, who was busted for X and got twenty-five years with the state. Gino was a tough mobster type who could do time with no problem, but she wasn't even trying to be tough. Hell, she was a girl.

Agent Pratt stood and greeted her when she entered his small office. "Good to see you, Jennifer."

She smiled but didn't say anything.

"So how was your day?"

"It's just beginning."

"Please have a seat." Mark pulled a chair out for her.

Jennifer sat down and crossed her legs. "Do you have any water or something to drink?"

"Will bottled water work?"

"That will be fine. I'm just a little thirsty, that's all."

Mark left and Jennifer examined many pictures of him throughout the office. Most were pictures of him and an older man. Jennifer assumed that the man was Mark's father. There were pictures of Mark at his college graduation and pictures of him playing little league baseball. It was obvious to Jennifer that Agent Pratt had come from a stable family, unlike many African-Americans she'd come in contact with.

Mark returned with the water, and Agent Ken Clarkson joined them. "Hello, Jennifer."

"Him again." He wondered what led her to be with a drug dealer.

"Jennifer … I'm your friend." Ken smiled then grabbed a yellow legal pad from Mark's file cabinet.

"Yeah, whatever."

Ken pulled up a chair and sat beside her, legal pad resting on his lap. "Okay, Jennifer, let's start with Twin."

Jennifer took a deep breath.

"Jennifer, you don't want to talk about Twin?"

"Well, Twin is my man."

"You wanna get tried for that ecstasy? I'm telling you, the judges ain't nice to cute little blonde white girls anymore, especially when it comes to ecstasy. Trust me, Jennifer, we can send you away for at least ten years."

"Let me start with Tommy—he's the Big Man."

"Who the hell is he?"

"I think his name is Tommy Dupree. They call him Fatboy."

Mark's eyes lit up. "I've been investigating him for about two years."

"Yeah, he's the man," Jennifer said. "He has the big house on the lake, Porsches, Benzes and shit..."

"So you work for Tommy?" Ken asked.

"No, I work for Twin."

"Twin works for Tommy?"

"Not exactly. I mean, Tommy has the most money and the connection. Twin doesn't work for him."

"So it's Twin, Tommy, and…who else in this little crew?"

"JoJo … Joe Ingram."

Ken scribbled on the legal pad.

Mark stood and paced. "Do you think you could help us get some audio on Tommy or Twin? I've been trying to get him ever since we closed the book on Jamal Stewart."

"Hell no. I'm not wearing a wire. Are you fuckin crazy? If Twin discovers me doing some shit like that he will kill me."

"We will be near to make sure everything goes okay."

"I'm not wearing a wire. That is final."

"So you'd rather go to prison."

"Yes, of course I would rather go to prison than get killed." Jennifer stood. "I don't know why I came in here in the first place. I should have gotten myself an attorney."

"Jennifer, sit down. You don't need an attorney, and you don't have to wear a wire," Ken said.

"What we need are the phone numbers of these people," Mark added.

"Twin's number is 555-0563."

"Who is the service provider?"

"Nextel."

"Twin's real name is…?" Ken asked.

Jennifer hesitated. She thought about how good Twin had been to her. She thought about the diamonds, the furs, and the luxury cars that he'd bought her over the years. But then she thought about the ten years she would get for the ecstasy. "Brandon. Brandon Agurs."

CHAPTER 5

Mark cupped one of Jennifer's huge breasts then put the other in his mouth. He moved his tongue down her stomach, into her navel, between her inner thigh ... She bit down hard on his neck. His manhood was now throbbing, but before he could slide it inside her, he came.

Then he woke from his dream and looked down at his boxers. He couldn't believe he was dreaming about a stripper. He sprang from his bed. It was three in the morning and he had semen in his boxers. In the next five minutes, he cleaned himself up and got back in the bed. He couldn't sleep. Instead he thought about Jennifer, not in a sexual way, but he wondered what led her to be with a drug dealer, what made her take off her clothes for a living.

Why is she on ecstasy? It was obvious the girl had problems, and he could tell she wasn't a bad person but that she'd made some bad decisions in life. Mark wanted to help her but didn't know why. Maybe because he was somewhat attracted to her. He told himself that he had to keep it on a professional level. After all, she was a crook, one of the bad guys.

*****

Twin met Jennifer with a hug and they kissed passionately. He picked her up and carried her to the sofa where he unbuttoned her blouse.

"Stop."

Twin looked confused. "What's the matter?"

"Nothing. Just that I wanted to talk to you first."

Twin buttoned her blouse back up. "You look worried. What's wrong?"

"You remember the girls that were in Miami with us? The one who you had me call the cops on?"

"Yeah."

"They told the DEA about you and me."

"How do you know that?"

Jennifer looked away briefly before resuming eye contact with Twin. "I had a little visit on my job. They know about the phone call that I made."

"What did they ask you?"

"They asked me about you and JoJo and Tommy."

"How the hell did they know about us?"

Again Jennifer looked away. "I don't know."

Twin grabbed her chin and forced her to look at him. "Let me find out you've been ratting to the cops. I will kill you, white bitch. Do you understand me?"

"Daddy, I would never do anything to hurt you. They said they've been investigating Tommy for two years now."

Twin was no longer in the mood for sex.

*****

The crew decided to meet at *Outback Steakhouse*. Tommy was a little hesitant to meet with Twin at first. After all, he'd gotten robbed and Twin had acted as if he didn't give a fuck about the whole incident. But when Twin had called, he said that it was important that they meet.

When they got to the restaurant, they were seated in a booth in the back. They all ordered *Heinekens*. Nobody wanted to eat.

"Okay, what is so important?" Tommy asked.

"Jennifer said the feds came to the club, and they were asking questions about us."

Tommy sipped his beer. "How the fuck can the feds be asking questions about us to your girl. They don't know we know your girl?"

"You know the two girls got busted, remember, coming from Miami."

"Yeah, but those girls don't know us," JoJo said.

He'd made a good point. One Twin hadn't thought about when he had spoken to Jennifer. He looked at Tommy. "She said the feds told her they been investigating you for a while. They probably got photos of all of us. I don't know."

"You sure your girl ain't telling?" Tommy asked.

"Fuck you, Fatboy."

"Fuck you, nigga!" Tommy said.

"Fat-ass nigga. I'll hurt you."

"And your mom will be making funeral arrangements," Tommy smiled.

"That's why your bitch ass got robbed," Twin said as he pointed his finger at Tommy's face.

"Y'all keep this shit quiet and cut the bickering. We all we got. Remember, we've known each other since the sandbox, so we gotta stick together," JoJo said.

Twin huffed but offered Tommy his hand.

After a few seconds of contemplation, Tommy shook his hand.

"Okay. We need to change our phones and phone numbers," Twin said.

"There's a cat in the barbershop that comes around with hot phones; he can get them for us at a hundred dollars each," JoJo said.

"Cool," Tommy said.

"Are we all on the same page?" JoJo asked.

"I'm okay. I still don't trust his bitch, though," Tommy said.

Twin didn't say anything. He just stared at Tommy.

*****

Mark and Jennifer met at *Dean & Deluca* for coffee. She was looking incredible with a black tube dress and heels that revealed her freshly polished toes. Her blonde hair was flowing freely in the light morning breeze. She was unusually tan today—maybe from a tanning booth.

Mark found himself staring at her breasts.

"Why are you looking at me like that?" she asked.

"I don't know…" He hesitated.

She crossed her legs then took a sip of her coffee.

"So, what's new with the crew?"

"Nothing really."

"They got new phones, right?"

"Yes." She stirred her coffee then placed the little straw in her mouth. She'd left traces of lipstick around it. "How'd you guess?"

"The number you gave me has been disconnected. Happens quite a bit with drug dealers. They get phones for a month, change numbers, phone companies, and everything. I imagine it must be a horrible life, always looking over your shoulder."

Jennifer pulled out a pair of Channel sunglasses from her purse. The sunglasses covered much of her face. "I guess you're right."

"You don't know, huh?"

"I mean, the life is like you're living on the edge, but it has its rewards."

His eyebrows rose. "Rewards? What kind of rewards?"

She held up her ring. "Five carats."

"Impressive." He sipped his bottled water.

"You think so?"

"Yes, I would have to save for two years to buy a ring like that."

"Two years!"

"Yes."

"It would probably take me two as well." She smiled.

"But Twin and the crew could buy it on sight, huh?" Mark said.

"Let's not talk about Twin." She placed her index finger over his mouth. "So, why do you do what you do? I know it's not for the money."

"I want to make a difference—for the kids and the elderly."

"Twin, JoJo, and Tommy aren't bad guys, you know?"

"Most drug dealers aren't."

"So why do you want to lock people up and take them away from their family? Now *that* must be a horrible life."

"Not really. I take pride in my job."

Jennifer looked at her watch. "Shit! I really have to be going now."

"So soon?"

"What was the purpose of this meeting, anyway? Why did you want to see me?"

"Just wanted to see that pretty face." He smiled.

"Really?"

"Yes. That ... and to find out Twin's new number."

There was a long silence, and then their eyes met and held. "704-555-0234," she finally said.

"Thank you, Jennifer. I will call you later." Mark scribbled the number on a napkin.

*****

Nia had reserved a room at the Holiday Inn downtown. As soon as JoJo walked in the room at noon, she unzipped his pants and grabbed his penis. He didn't resist. After he was aroused he picked her up and carried her to the bed. There he pulled her G-cut undies down with his teeth and trailed her belly with his tongue before tasting her wet vagina. She grabbed his head. "This pussy is yours."

Moments later, he was pushing his penis in as far as it would go.

"Yeah, muthafucka! I want you to fuck the shit out of me."

He turned her over on her stomach and plunged hard. He slapped her ass.

She bit down on the pillow and yelled, "Harder!"

They went at it for twenty minutes. She'd ridden him. He'd sexed her from the spoon position to the missionary position. She had tears streaming down her face now.

JoJo stood and put on his boxers.

Nia looked at his body and smiled. He had a basketball player's frame—tall, lean, abs as solid as steel. She loved the way he made her feel. He stimulated her physically as well as mentally.

He turned and smiled at her.

She just lay there, unwilling to move, the sheet half covering her naked body.

He walked over and yanked it away.

"What the hell are you doing?"

"Why are you just lying there? What are you thinking about?"

"I was just thinking that maybe me and you should run away; you know, blow this spot. I mean I hate this life of being a hustler's wife. I feel like one of those chicks in a Vickie Stringer or Danielle Santiago novel. There has to be more to life than this."

He looked toward the window. "I know. This shit has gotten old to me, too."

She licked her lips. "I want you, JoJo. I want you all to myself."

He contemplated something before saying, "You know that can't be possible. I mean, you have a man—my best friend at that."

"Come on. Get off that best friend bull shit. If he was really your best friend you wouldn't be fuckin me."

"I don't like this shit." He put his shirt on and buttoned it. "I can't go on like this, and I feel bad every time we have sex. And now you done went and caught feelings and shit ... I thought this was just supposed to be a fuck thing and nothing more."

Nia rose from the bed and picked up her undergarments from the floor, shoving them in her overnight bag. "I know I'm not supposed to catch feelings, but I enjoy being with you, and the dick *is* good." She smiled.

"I know I got skills. Right?"

"I've had better." She blushed and revealed her dimples.

"Yeah, right. That's why your ass is talking about running away with me."

She stepped into the bathroom, still completely naked.

JoJo's eyes zeroed in on her ass.

"JoJo, come and take a shower with me," she teased.

"I don't want to."

"Why not?"

"'Cause I'm going to wanna hit that ass again."

"As if that would be a bad thing."

JoJo kicked his boots off and stepped into the bathroom.

Nia was on her knees, her mouth open, waiting on him.

Chapter 6

"Listen, Tommy..." Alicia glanced over her shoulder. "I have to be going."

"Can I call you?" He leaned against the glass door of the nail shop.

"Sure, that's why I gave you the number. But at this point, I can only see us being friends."

"Why?"

"I think you're a drug dealer."

"How do you figure?"

She looked over at his Escalade but didn't say anything.

"The truck, huh?"

"I've dated hustlers before."

"What happened?"

"They usually go to jail or get killed by rival drug dealers."

"I'll call you, Alicia. Maybe you can help me rewrite that ending."

"Call me, Tommy. It was nice meeting you."

*****

Tommy and Nia sat on the sofa, counting money, putting it in thousand-dollar stacks—hundred-dollar bills on top then the twenties, tens and fives ... After they finished counting the money they stuffed it into Samsonite briefcases. The money totaled about two hundred thousand dollars. Nia got up and peered out the window. A peaceful street in suburbia, with SUV's and European cars in every driveway. Nothing eventful ever happened on this street.

Tommy watched Nia carefully. "What's wrong?"

She shrugged. "I don't know, Tommy; I guess all this money in here is making me nervous. Somebody has to know about you."

"Why do you say that?"

"Tommy, you just got robbed a week ago. You know the old saying in the street: If the niggas know, the police know."

Tommy walked over and hugged Nia.

"Tommy, I don't know if I can go on like this anymore. I was telling my friend the other day that I feel like I'm in one of those street lit books."

"What books?"

"You know ... *A Hustler's Wife, Little Ghetto Girl*..."

"Listen, baby, this ain't no book. This is real life."

Her eyes had expanded. "I know, but I can't help the fact that I'm scared."

"There's nothing to be afraid of. You, of all people, don't have anything to worry about. I would never involve you in my life. I remember what happened to Jamal and how he had his girl on the run with him and shit. I ain't that kind of nigga."

Their eyes met and held.

"Listen, I have a goal. As soon as I make my goal, I'm out of this shit; I'm finished with this lifestyle forever. I promise, babe."

Nia walked over and grabbed the briefcase. "Tommy, two hundred thousand dollars is in here; why ain't this enough? You have no kids and you are not married. Why ain't that enough?"

Tommy considered it. He did have a lot of money, and he could probably do a lot with it. He'd thought about a legitimate profession, like running car lots, and investing in real estate, but he hadn't pursued it.

"Tommy, I know we aren't the ideal couple. I mean, our sex is horrible ... but, Tommy, you have such a big heart and you are such a good person ... I don't want anything to happen to you."

"Nothing is going to happen to me. See, a lot of people go outside their crews and that's when shit gets ugly for them. Me, Twin, and JoJo have been knowing each other since the sandbox. I know those are my niggas."

Nia sat down while Tommy went in the room and got another bag full of money. They continued to count.

When they finished, there was a total of four hundred thousand dollars in the house.

*****

When Tommy and Twin got off the plane at the Miami International Airport, two men in plain clothes met them.

"Tommy and Brandon?" the taller of the two men called out.

Tommy stared without saying a word.

Twin looked at the two men then said, "Who the fuck are you?"

The shorter of the two agents flashed his badge. "I'm agent Rawls and this is my partner. We're with DEA, Miami division."

"Yeah? And what do you want with us?" Tommy asked nervously.

"We just want to talk."

"About what?"

"Follow us. We'll go somewhere private. Do you boys drink coffee?"

"Are we under arrest?"

"No. Just want to ask some questions."

"We don't know shit about drugs. All I know is they're bad for you," Twin said.

The tall agent laughed. "It's funny you would say that, Brandon, because according to our information, you've done time for drugs already. Remember that possession case when the police raided your girlfriend's apartment and found those five ounces of coke?"

"Yeah, but I've done my time for that. We need to get our bags and head to the beach. We're on vacation."

"From what? You don't have jobs."

"We have to be going." Tommy said, sidestepping the two officers.

"Listen, I want you to take heed to this warning: You have to be lucky all your life, but we only have to be lucky once. Drug dealers always slip up."

"Have a good day officers."

*****

Manny met Tommy in the lobby of his hotel. They greeted one another with a hug.

"Let's go somewhere for drinks," Manny said.

"Not right now."

Manny looked confused. "We always go for drinks. What's wrong?"

"The feds approached us when we got off the plane."

Manny laughed. "And you are worried, huh?"

"Hell yeah, man. I don't want no part of those mothafuckas."

"You know how many times I've been approached by the feds? I don't give a damn about them. If they lock me up, I'm going to get out. If they charge me, I'll have the best attorneys money can buy. If I go to jail, my family will still be taken care of," Manny said confidently. "I have my lawyer's number on speed dial."

Tommy relaxed. He'd known Manny for quite some time, and he admired his knowledge of the drug trade. He knew Manny would advise him wisely. Manny and his family had been in the business for years, and they were all very wealthy. Tommy wanted to get where Manny was—living in the mansions, driving the Ferraris and Bentleys. He knew that if he ever stocked a few million dollars, he would get out of the drug game in a hurry.

Manny put his arm around Tommy. "Come on, man. Let's go to the bar and talk. We can't let the feds stop our show. I don't know about you, but I got a lot of people depending on me."

Outside, Manny gave fifty dollars to the valet, who quickly retrieved the Ferrari.

The beach wasn't crowded. Manny sped down Collins Avenue until he got to Lincoln, where they found the Moon Room, a private restaurant. The guy at the door smiled at Manny and led him to a room in the back. Young Latino women with their breasts exposed and tight skirts waited the tables while salsa music played in the background

"What the hell is this place?" Tommy asked, amazed.

"This is my favorite restaurant. All the girls in here are hookers, so if you see one you like you can take her upstairs and screw her."

Tommy had seen several attractive women as soon as he'd walked in the door. However, it would be downright shameful if he couldn't get an erection for some pussy that he would have to pay for. "I just want something to drink."

The waitress appeared in a black skirt with red pasties over her nipples. "Hey, Manny." She smiled. "Do you want the usual?"

"Hey, Anna, this is my friend Tommy. Get him what he wants."

Anna walked over to Tommy's side of the table, pressing her 36 D's against his shoulders. "What can I get you to drink?"

"Vodka and cranberry juice."

"Grey goose okay?"

"Fine," Tommy told Anna.

"I'll take a glass of wine, Anna. Give me your finest white wine," Manny said.

Salsa music continued to play in the background, and Tommy

thought about the movie Scarface. Here he was—a boy from North Carolina, in a restaurant with beautiful, topless waitresses and talking to a man with cartel connections.

"So, Tommy... are we going to do business or what?"

Tommy thought hard. He knew that the feds were onto him. He knew that he couldn't send the product back on the plane. "I have no way of getting my product back."

"For five thousand dollars extra, I will have my people bring it to you," Manny said. "Like I said, nothing is going to stop this show. I have inventory and it has to be moved."

Tommy's eyes lit up. "You could get that done?"

"Come on, Tommy, we're family. This is what family is for."

Anna brought their drinks and two complimentary Cuban cigars.

Manny passed Tommy a cigar. "You smoke cigars, don't you?"

"No."

"You're a big boy now. Smoke ... or at least pretend you're smoking it."

Tommy put the cigar in his mouth. He really felt like he was a part of a cartel. But he knew, at this level it was deep involvement. He knew he just couldn't up and quit if he wanted to. He would have to disappear.

Manny smiled then slapped Anna on her ass.

*****

"Twin, I think we should chill," Fatboy said, speaking into his cell phone. He glanced at the Charlotte Coliseum as he drove by in his Escalade.

"Why?"

"Your girl told you they were on to us. And that little confrontation in the airport..."

"Nigga, don't worry about that shit. That's just probably some security type shit. Remember 9-11, nigga? Ain't nobody safe at the airports."

"That was the DEA that stopped us, nigga; that wasn't security."

"We're okay, man. Don't worry about that shit."

"Take it easy on these phones."

"The phones are okay. We just got them. Remember?"

"Well, you can never be too sure."

"I don't want to chill; I need to make money."

"I need money, too."

"Nigga, you got to have at least a million dollars."

"I wish, Twin."

"But you got money for the best lawyers, just in case some shit goes down."

"I don't put my trust in lawyers. That's how niggas go to the pen."

"Fatboy, let's make one more run."

"One more?"

"Yeah."

"I guess we can since Manny seems to think it's going to be okay."

"Manny said it was okay then its okay. He's been doing this shit a whole lot longer than we have."

"You think so?"

"I know so, man. Relax and let's get this money as long as we can."

CHAPTER 7

Tommy's phone record indicated that he'd recently talked to Manny Alvarez. Mark made a call to DEA, Miami division, and ran Alvarez's name by the agent-in-charge, Mario Santiallas.

Santiallas had forwarded the call to Matthew Donahue, the agent that had been investigating Manny for the past three years.

"Alvarez is supplying North Carolina?" Mark asked.

"Actually, Alvarez isn't his real name, but it's been his name for the past six months. His real name is Manny Gomez, but Alvarez is his alias. We're watching him, and we're watching your guys when they come into town."

"Really?" Mark said. Then he turned Manny's picture over.

"Yes. Gomez is major. He's supplying Tennessee, Georgia, Louisiana, and Virginia, New York, and New Jersey."

"Yes, that's serious."

"Does he talk on phones?"

"He has several phones, and he rarely says anything except suggesting a meeting for drinks."

"I guess he's gonna be a tough one, huh?"

"Actually, I think we're onto something. We've just pinched his Louisiana guy with ten kilos, and he's being helpful."

"Singing, huh?"

"The next American Idol."

Mark laughed. "So if you set Manny up, what do you think he'll do?"

"I don't know. These situations can be tough when it's a family organization. I don't think he'll rat on his family as long as he can still make moves from inside."

"Will he be able to do that?"

"Manny is powerful; we estimate he's moving at least five thousand kilos a week."

"Yeah, your guy is major. Keep me posted on his status."

"You bet," Donahue said.

Mark terminated the call.

*****

Alicia and Tommy met in front of Gold's gym. She wore Nike running shoes, no socks, and tight nylon shorts that revealed her muscular legs. Tommy couldn't help but stare, and he couldn't wait for her to turn around so he could see her backside. He got an erection just looking at Alicia, something he hadn't been able to do in a while.

They walked to the desk together, and she told the attendant that Tommy was her guest for the day.

First they went to the bench. She worked out with a hundred pounds. Her objective was noy to bulk up but remain toned and defined.

Tommy walked around the gym. He felt out of place. Not that he hadn't been accustomed to working out, but he just wasn't in shape. He scanned the gym. Most of the patrons were white, and they came in all sizes—thin, fat, short, and even pudgy like him. By far, out of all the women, Alicia had the best body. He went to the water fountain twice, trying to kill some time, and hoped Alicia wasn't going to ask him to get on the bench press. But it happened on his fourth trip from the water fountain.

"Tommy, I hope you ain't just planning on watching me."

"Actually, I *was* just planning on watching today."

"Wrong. If you're going to be in my presence, you're going to have to get yourself in some kind of shape." She walked over to him and nudged his belly.

"I got a stomach of steel." He laughed then rubbed his belly.

"That's really sad that you're proud of that gut. You act like a redneck trucker or something."

Tommy put another hundred pounds on the bench. The total was now two hundred pounds.

"Since you haven't worked out in a while, you might want to go light."

Tommy laughed then added ten more pounds to each side of the bar. "I ain't no weakling, baby. I'm almost 250 pounds. You don't think I can lift two hundred pounds?"

"I'm going to spot you," Alicia said.

46

Tommy lay on the bench then started rubbing his belly.

She laughed then asked, "What are you doing?"

"Rubbing my good luck charm. This is where I get my strength." He took the bar off the rack and pumped out three quick repetitions. But on his fourth rep, he struggled a little, barely managing to finish. The fifth rep was a little different. He was terribly hang gliding before Alicia helped him put the weight back on the rack.

Tommy stood, completely out of breath. "You shouldn't have helped me. I had it," he managed to say.

Alicia laughed aloud. "Yeah, right. If I hadn't stepped in, you would've killed yourself."

Tommy walked over to the water fountain again, gulped some more water, and then walked back over to the bench. He didn't attempt any more chest exercises. Instead he watched Alicia for the remainder of her workout.

"So, Tommy... you gonna run with me?"

"Hell no. I can't even run a mile."

"If you want to go out on a date with me, you're gonna have to run with me." Alicia smiled.

Tommy thought long and hard. He knew he wasn't in shape and he thought about all the water he'd had. He would probably throw up if he tried to run. He looked at Alicia again, who was smiling brightly. Then he looked at her legs. *Damn, this woman is fine.* He could feel his erection coming on again. Damned if he knew why she could easily arouse him. No woman had ever gotten him hard just by looking at him. For a brief instance, he imagined himself between those muscular legs, humping away.

"Tommy, what are you going to do? Are you going to get on the treadmill with me or not?"

"I'm going. What do you think; I'm a punk or something?"

"Cool. I like your spirit. Tommy, you are okay with me."

Alicia got on the treadmill and Tommy got on the one behind her. She set her speed to where she would run her miles at twelve-minute intervals. Tommy set his speed for eighteen-minute miles. He held on to the rail as he walked fast, then he began a light trot.

Alicia was wide open, *iPod* attached to her arm. She was free. Nobody could stop her.

*****

Night had fallen. Alicia and Tommy talked in the gym parking lot. He stood in front of her while she leaned up against her Toyota Camry. He looked into her eyes and, for the first time, noticed that they were hazel. "You have the most amazing eyes."

She smiled then said, "Thanks."

"So, Ms. Jane Fonda, are we going out or what?"

She frowned. "I hope you don't think that's a compliment, comparing me to a white girl."

Tommy grabbed her hands. They were soft, and he loved them. "I didn't mean anything by that; I'm just saying, you all in shape and shit."

Alicia turned around. "Jane wishes she had a back like mine."

"Now ain't that the truth."

She giggled.

"What are you laughing at?" Tommy asked.

"Just thinking about you running on that treadmill. You was bent all over, cramping."

"Yeah, all that water I drank fucked me up."

She frowned. "Tommy, can you stop cursing so much?"

Tommy put his hands up in defense. "I'm sorry, ma'am, it's just that all the niggas that I'm around ... all we do is curse. I mean, there are certain people you just have to curse around to get your point across. You know what I mean?"

"I guess."

He put his hand in hers again. "So are we going out again or what?"

She pulled a towel from her gym bag and wiped her face. She didn't answer him.

"Okay, Alicia. You have me damn near kill myself by getting on that fucking treadmill, and now we can't go out?"

"Tommy, you're cursing again."

"Sorry."

She looked at him then started laughing again. "Tommy, I'll go out with you. You don't have to look so mad."

"No bullshit—I mean ..."

"Yes, of course I will. You went out of your way to please me. I like that a lot about you."

Tommy hadn't anticipated her going out with him on a date. He figured a girl like Alicia was way out of his league—and she was. She was cute; he wasn't. She was in shape; he definitely was not that. He didn't know where he would take her. He thought about asking her to go fishing but quickly dismissed the thought. She was too cute for that.

"So, Tommy, when and where are we going?"

"I don't know. What would you like to do?"

She frowned. "Come on, Tommy. You're supposed to know those types of things. Women like men who has everything all planned out. Women like men to take control. Come on, Tommy, be a man."

"Well, I don't know. Let me surprise you."

She smiled then wiped her face again. "I like surprises."

"Let's go out Friday."

"Friday is good."

*****

Mark Pratt pretended that the crumpled paper was a basketball and that he was shooting a three-pointer.

Ken Clarkson blocked Mark's game-winning three-pointer. "Get that outta here." He was happy to have blocked the shot because he knew he could only do that in the office. On the basketball court, he'd never beat Mark, never block his shot, never steal the ball from him, and never dunk on him. All of which Mark had done to him at will.

Ken continued his little celebration.

Then the phone rang. "Agent Pratt speaking."

"How's it going, Pratt? This is Agent Donahue of the Miami Division. I got news for you. We busted your boy Manny Gomez."

"Oh yeah? How did that happen? I was thinking he was Mr. Untouchable."

"A guy who'd grown up with his family just got a conscience. He knew that he was under investigation along with Gomez. He was scared. Came in and began talking, then he called an attorney and asked for immunity. We wired him up and sent him to make a buy from Gomez. We then raided the house and seized a hundred kilos of pure Colombian coke."

CHAPTER 8

The U.S. Marshals brought Manny Gomez into an interrogation room. When they took the cuffs off him, he lunged at Agent Donahue, reaching for his throat.

Manny was quickly restrained and shoved into a corner. His head hit the cement wall. He bounced up and spat at a Marshal.

The big man grabbed Manny by his head and tossed him back to the floor.

"Fuck you. Fuck all you bastards!" Manny said.

"So, Manny, I take it that you don't want to help yourself out of this jam," Donahue said.

"Fuck you, you stinking pig. Haven't you done enough? You've ruined my life."

"Manny, you ruined your own life."

"Who the hell are the two new goons?" Manny asked as he looked at Mark and Ken.

"These are my fellow officers from North Carolina. They are here to ask you a few questions."

Manny's eyebrows rose. "Is that so?"

"Yes. Do you know Tommy Dupree?"

"Yes ... Maybe ... Depends."

"Are you his supplier?"

"No, George Bush is his supplier, and he's mine too." Manny remained on the floor, looking up.

Donahue walked over.

Manny spat on him then bit his shin.

Donahue grabbed Manny's neck and choked him.

The two Marshals broke up the fight.

"Fuck you. I'll never do your job for you."

"Manny, you're gonna die in jail."

"I don't give a fuck, as long as my family is taken care of. And guess what, buddy, my son is fifteen years old and he can spend a million dollars a year until he turns seventy five. Can you say that about your kids?"

"No, but I can go home to my kids," Donahue bragged.

Manny laughed a loud, wicked laugh. "You guys are really fucking annoying. I try to give you valuable information about your president, but you don't want to follow up on it. But if I say something about Tommy, a great guy who has nothing, you'll put him away for years. See what a corrupt system we have here?"

"Manny you're a really charming guy," Mark Pratt said.

"And you really are a slave of the system, man. Don't you understand what they are doing to Blacks and Latinos?"

"Manny, I've heard it all. I'm not in the mood for the Black-and-Latino shit."

"Fuck you. You're a pig, just like the rest of them. Take me back to my cell."

"Stand him up," Donahue said.

The U.S. Marshals stood Manny up. He and Donahue made eye contact. They stared at each other for a long time. "Okay, Manny, I'm going to give you one more chance. Tell me who is your supplier and who are you supplying?"

"George Bush is my supplier, and I'm supplying DEA Agent Donahue and his two friends."

"Get this disgusting bastard out of my face," Donahue said. "He'll come around soon enough."

*****

When Alicia opened the door to her apartment, she was wearing a form-fitting dress.

Tommy's eyes were immediately drawn to her thighs.

When she saw him staring, she blushed a little.

"I feel like I'm dressed too casual."

"How's that?"

"Jeans and boots. You looking like you about to walk down the red carpet or something."

She laughed. "Well, a fashionista has to look her best."

"A *fashionista*? What the hell is that?"

She giggled. "Tommy, you're funny. Come on inside."

Tommy walked in and sat on her couch. "You don't mind if I sit down, do you?"

"You're already sitting; what are you talking about?"

"I guess I am," Tommy said, his eyes moving back to her thighs.

"Tommy, you're looking at me like I'm a pork chop or something."

"I ... just didn't expect you to be looking like this, that's all."

"Well, Tommy, when you saw me the first time, I was dressed down. Then it was the gym; I don't get dressed up for the gym," she said. She walked past him with a slow, seductive walk.

"So where are we going? I got us some appointments for massages."

"Come on, Tommy. It's seven at night, and I don't want to go for massages. Let's go to dinner."

"Where?"

"*The Palm.*"

"*The Palm* ... sounds expensive."

"Yeah, it is kind of pricey, but I can pay for my own meal." She winked.

Tommy felt a little insulted. Who in the hell did she think he was? He had money, and he could afford any restaurant in Charlotte. He pulled out a big wad of cash. "You'll never pay for your own meal when you're with me."

Her eyes stretched. "Tommy! Rule number one: If you're going to be a drug dealer ... at least be smart about it."

*****

"Give me an apple martini," Alicia told the young waitress.

"Hennessey, straight," Tommy ordered.

The waitress disappeared. Two minutes later, she returned with the drinks, and took their orders.

Tommy ordered the New York strip, and Alicia had the broiled salmon.

He made eye contact with her. He knew she was special. For starters, he could get an erection just by looking at her. Also ... Well ... that was more than enough. He could look at her forever. She was a good girl, and he longed to have a woman like her.

He began to think about the other side of his life—the street life. He thought about the next trip to Miami. He thought about the adrenaline rush he got from counting money. He had plenty, but he didn't have happiness. But he was happy for the moment.

"Tommy, what are you thinking about?"

He cut his steak in small portions, thinking about how he should answer her question. He sure as hell didn't want her to know that he was thinking about the streets. He finally looked up at her and smiled. "I was just thinking about us."

Alicia smiled. "What about us?"

"I think we have chemistry."

"We do. But, Tommy, I told you I can't see us being more than friends unless you stop hustling."

"Why are you so set against dating hustlers?"

"Actually, Tommy, my father sold drugs for many years, and it afforded me many things like ballet lessons, private schools, expensive cars, and more."

Tommy was amazed. He never imagined Alicia being from a family involved with crime or anything remotely illegal. He thought her father might have been some big-time executive or attorney, some- one who couldn't possibly understand the plight of the poor and underprivileged. "Just out of curiosity, what made your dad stop hustling?"

"His best friend got caught. The feds gave him life and charged him as a kingpin. My mom begged him to stop because she didn't want to lose him to the system."

"So his best friend didn't rat him out?"

"No. They were like brothers. Daddy still takes good care of him. He sends him money, visits him once a month, and takes care of his wife and kids."

"What a story." Tommy sipped his *Hennessey*.

"Tommy, what's even more amazing ... Daddy hasn't sold drugs in eight years, but he's made close to ten million dollars in the last three years."

Tommy's eyebrows rose. "Doing what?"

"Real estate investing. He's invested in commercial real estate."

"I wish I could do something like that."

"Tommy..." Alicia lowered her voice. "Take a look around. What do you see?"

Tommy scanned the restaurant. He shrugged. "People, I guess."

"Tommy, most of these people in here have money. And guess what ... a lot of them didn't get it honestly."

"You know I always think that anyway, Alicia. I just thought that was my twisted mind."

Alicia sipped her martini. "Let me tell you something. Everybody that has money didn't get it being honest. Most people steal somehow or another."

Tommy couldn't believe they shared an ideology. She appeared to be so naive. "How do you think these people got their money?"

"That, I don't know. Drugs, maybe, or some kind of white-collar crime ... My understanding is that very few get it honestly."

"Your point is...?" Tommy said, then leaned closer, placing his forearms on the table. "I thought you were against hustling."

"My point is...make your money and get out."

"Like your daddy did?"

"Exactly."

Her smiled was innocent. Her eyes seemed to being saying she had ideas that could take him to the top—unlike Nia, who could never tell him anything. Nia was against him selling drugs most of the time, but when it came to her wants, they had to be fulfilled at all cost.

"I don't know real estate."

"Tommy, you can learn anything, and you can do anything you put your mind to. You think my daddy knew the real estate game?"

Tommy was silent for a moment, absorbing it all. He knew he was very capable of learning, but the drug money came so easy.

"Tommy, you can do anything. I haven't known you but for a couple of weeks, and you appear to be a very intelligent man."

"Alicia, do you think your dad can teach me how to make money with real estate?"

"I don't know, but we can ask him. I'll call him," Alicia said, then dug into her purse and pulled out her cell phone.

"Daddy!" she said. Her face lit up.

Tommy looked on with envy. He'd never known his dad—only his stepdad, who was serving a lengthy sentence.

Alicia said, "Dad, I'm with my friend here, Tommy, and he does the same thing you used to do and he was wondering if you could help him invest his money in real estate." She listened for a few seconds then passed Tommy the phone.

The man on the other end of the phone said, "Tommy."

"Yes. I mean ... Yes, sir."

"Forget that *sir* shit. You can call me Don."

Tommy relaxed and laughed.

"Tommy, I hear you are playing a dangerous game."

"I guess you can say that," Tommy said, then looked at Alicia.

"Tommy, I ain't knocking your life, but you have to be prepared when the Grim Reaper comes."

"The Grim Reaper? What do you mean?"

"The police. Man, I hope you ain't that naïve."

"I just had never heard them referred to as the Grim Reaper."

"Tommy, I'm from the old school, man, but you know what I mean."

"Yeah, I know what you mean." At that moment Tommy thought about his stepdad. Thought about how he looked in the visitation room. Prison was a sad place, where people got old and sick. There was nothing to look forward to, and there was so much barbed wire. He knew that if he were ever locked up, he would go absolutely crazy.

"But like I was saying, Tommy, you're playing a serious game, a game where you could lose your life. That's what I mean by the Grim Reaper."

"I got you."

"No, I got *you*. Obviously my daughter likes you, if she wants me to help you get out of your situation."

Tommy smiled then glanced at Alicia. He really felt love for her now.

"So, Tommy, if you could come out to California, I can show you what I got going on, and maybe you'll see the light."

"Cool. I would love to come out there. I've never been to Cali." All of his teeth were exposed when he smiled. He knew at that moment he wanted Alicia to be his wife. He'd never met anyone who believed in him.

*****

When Tommy pulled up to Alicia's apartment complex, the sun had gone down. The moon was full, and very few stars decorated the pitch black sky. He parked in front of her building and turned on the radio. Usher hummed in the background. "I hope you had a good time," Tommy said.

"Actually, I did. It doesn't take much for me."

He turned and faced her. "I really like you."

She smiled but didn't say anything.

"I *really* like you."

"So did you have a good time?" she asked.

"Yeah, of course I did, because I was with someone I wanted to be with."

"And who might that be?" she asked, then flung her hair over her shoulder.

He didn't answer; he just leaned toward her and gave her a small peck on the lip. His erection was growing.

When he pulled away, her eyes were still closed, as if she were expecting a long, passionate kiss. "I want you to go fishing with me," he said.

"Fishing?"

"Yes. It should be fun."

"I've never been fishing before. I'll have to think about it."

"What is it to think about? I have a boat. You will love it. Trust me."

"First of all, I just got my hair done. Second, I don't want to be smelling like fish."

"You're such a woman."

"But that's what you love, right?" Their eyes met.

His heart began to beat fast. His erection throbbed. He leaned toward her and kissed her. Their lips locked and his tongue entered her mouth.

He pulled away. "So, are you going to go with me or not?"

She blushed, revealing deep dimples. "Only one condition."

"What's that?"

"If you paint my fishing pole pink."

"Pink? You've gotta be kidding."

"I'm a girl, remember? I likely girly things."

"You may be a girl, but in that gym you're Iron Woman."

She laughed. "Yes, but still I'm a girl."

"I'll think about that pink fishing pole thing."

"Okay... think about it. I have to be getting some sleep. I have an accounting class in the morning."

He pulled her toward him and gave her one more kiss. His penis tried to break free.

CHAPTER 9

"**H**ave either of you ever thought about investing in real estate?" Tommy asked Twin and JoJo. They were at Twin's apartment, sitting at his kitchen table.

"You mean like buying old houses and fixing them up?" JoJo asked.

Twin looked at Tommy. "Why you asking this shit?"

"I may know of an opportunity."

"What kind?" JoJo asked.

"This broad I've been seeing... her daddy deals with real estate and shit, out in Cali, and I'm supposed to talk to him and see if we can clean up this dirty money."

"Okay, we're trying to be legit now?" Twin said. "We're trying to get out of the drug game after we wash the money?"

Tommy hesitated. He didn't really want to answer the question. He didn't want Twin and JoJo to think he was getting soft. He wanted them to think that he would run the streets as long as they did.

"Nigga, this girl you met influencing the shit out of you. When are we going to see this broad?" Twin asked, laughing.

"Naw, nigga. Can't nobody influence me. I'm just getting smart, that's all."

"Shit. Seems like you want to get all legit all of a sudden. You meet a broad and it's *let's try some real estate* shit. Nigga, do you know that no real business is gonna pay like this?" JoJo asked.

Tommy decided that there was no use in trying to show them another way.

*****

Mark found himself in a dark corner in the back of the Uptown Carousel.

A small busty black girl approached him. "You wanna dance?"

"No, I'm fine."

"Yes, you are." She sat on Mark's lap.

"Would you mind getting off me?"

She frowned. "So what are you in here for if you don't want entertainment?"

"Just to get a drink."

"Nigga, you drinking water," the woman said, glancing at the bottled water in front of him.

"Listen, can you just leave me alone? I'm not bothering anybody."

"Oh… stuck-up-ass nigga. I bet you got a small dick, anyhow," the woman said as she walked away.

"Next entertainer up is Jennifer," the DJ announced. *Pop That Thang* by Christina Millian was played. When Jennifer walked on stage, two black guys, two white guys, and a Hispanic—all with money in their hands—surrounded the stage.

Jennifer walked to the edge and stood in front of the Mexican, pulled her thong aside, and ordered him to give up the handful of cash.

One of the black guys moved closer.

Jennifer walked seductively across the stage then looked back. With her finger, she signaled for one of the guys to follow her. They all scrambled and made their way to the other side of the stage, where she got down on all fours. One by one they all relinquished their cash.

Then another set of guys came up during the second song. By the time she'd finished dancing the stage was covered with cash. One of the bouncers brought a bag out to help her pick up all the money.

As she left the stage, she walked by Mark's table. "Hey, that was quite a performance you put on up there," Mark said.

"Oh, Mr. DEA, I didn't know you were here."

"Yeah, I've been here for a while."

She slid into the booth beside him. "Will you buy me a drink?" she asked.

"Jennifer, you just made at least three hundred dollars."

She frowned. "What is the world coming to when a guy can't buy a girl a drink?"

"No, it's not like that at all. I was just kidding you."

Jennifer smiled then flagged down the waitress and ordered a sex on the beach.

"So what brings you here?" Jennifer asked.

"I don't know. I guess I was kind of bored and didn't have anything else to do."

She giggled. "You just don't look like the type that would be hanging at a titty bar."

"Neither do you."

She frowned. "Well, Mr. Federal Agent, my life hasn't been all peaches and cream."

"Nobody's life has. That's only in the movies."

The waitress placed Jennifer's drink on the table. *Soldier* by Destiny's Child played in the background. Jennifer hummed along.

"So you like street guys, huh?" Mark inquired.

"Not necessarily."

"What kind of guys do you like?"

She sipped her drink, looked away for a moment, then said, "We are a bit inquisitive, aren't we?"

"Just conversation, that's all."

"I know. I'm just kidding with you, man. Don't be so uptight." She reached across the table and loosened his collar. "Come on, man, relax. I don't like stiff guys." She giggled. "I take that back. I like stiff guys, but not guys that act stiff."

"How did you and Twin meet?"

"We met in the mall. He walked up to me and told me to pick out anything in the mall and he would buy it."

Mark's eyebrow's rose. "So what did you do?"

"I went on a mini shopping spree. I spent maybe three or four thousand dollars."

"Does he make you happy?"

She looked away but didn't answer.

"He doesn't make you happy, does he?"

She drank the rest of her drink in one gulp. "You see, Mr. DEA, it isn't always about happiness; it's about what you know."

"I don't understand."

"I know you don't understand, and that's what I mean by stiff. You're a square. You're not a bad guy; you've never had rough times."

"I beg to differ."

"Listen to your grammar. Nobody in my circle would say that."

"Okay. Your point is?"

The waitress put two more drinks on the table—another sex on the beach and another bottled water.

"My point is that you had your parents growing up. They lived with you. My daddy molested me."

Mark didn't know what to say at first. Finally, he uttered, "Sorry."

"Twin never knew his father, and his mother sold ass to support him and his brother."

"Okay, I think I know what you're getting at," Mark said as he thought about his parents. He'd known all the time that he was fortunate to have such loving parents.

"My point is people have wounds, Agent Pratt, wounds from childhood that are hard to cover up. People are hurting, and we mask our hurt with material stuff like designer clothes, cars, and plastic surgery."

"I think I see where you're going."

"See … drug dealers and strippers are two of a kind, and they go together like peanut butter and jelly."

"But you are such a sweet girl. I just hate for you to be in this situation."

"And what situation is that?"

"Dancing for a living and dating a hustler."

"You can't save the world, agent." She stood from the table. "I'm a big girl. I can handle myself." She walked away.

Mark stared at her ass. He'd gotten an erection.

*****

"What the fuck is this lipstick doing on your collar, Motherfucker?" Nia pressed as she presented the shirt to Tommy.

"I don't know shit. I was drunk last night. I don't know how I got home."

She walked over to the bed and looked at Tommy with suspicion but didn't say a word.

"Listen, Nia, why don't you just get the fuck out of my face before I hurt you."

Nia threw the shirt at Tommy. "You ain't gonna do a goddamn thing. If you hit me, my brother will be over here so fast to whip your fat ass you won't know what hit you."

62

"And I promise you that nigga will get a free ride to the morgue. So if you want to spare your mama a funeral, you won't call that coward-ass nigga."

Nia picked up a pillow and hit Tommy with it. "You fat bastard. I know you're cheating on me."

"I told you, I was drunk. I can't remember what happened last night. How did I get home, anyway?"

"Nigga, you drove home," Nia said furiously.

Tommy's cell phone rang. He grabbed his pants that were on the floor and pulled the phone from a pocket. "Hello."

"Tommy, this is Hector, Manny's brother."

"What's up, Hector?"

"The police got Manny."

"Oh yeah?"

"Yeah. I'll tell you about it when you come down. Maybe we'll have drinks, okay?"

So many questions ran through Tommy's head. He wondered how Manny had gotten busted. He wanted to know what he'd gotten busted with. And there was the ultimate question: Was he cooperating with the police? Tommy got up and put his pants on. He started to pace.

"Where are you going?"

Tommy held his hand up to Nia's face. "Not now, Nia. I have other shit to worry about."

Nia saw that he was serious. "What happened, Tommy?"

"Manny, my supplier, has been busted."

"So what do you have to do with that?"

"Nothing. I'm concerned, that's all."

Their eyes met and held. Nobody said anything. He thought about Alicia and her father. He knew he had to make the trip to California. He had to find a better way.

*****

After Tommy left, Nia walked into the kitchen, picked up the cordless telephone, and called JoJo.

"I need to see you," she said.

"Why?"

She giggled a little. "I need to see my friend."

"Oh, you want to see Monster, huh?"

"Nigga, you ain't holding like that," she laughed. "But, yeah, I do need some dick."

"Where is Fatboy?"

"He left. He got some bad news today. Somebody name Manny got busted."

"Manny is our connect. Well, Tommy is the only one he deals with."

"I don't know where he went, but I'm glad, though. Now me and you can get away."

"You are a scandalous bitch."

"You like it, though."

JoJo was silent. He thought about what that would mean for him. The connect was in custody, and he didn't have any other way of making money. He didn't have the stash of money that Tommy had. He needed to talk to Tommy to find out the details.

"So, nigga, you going to fuck me or what?"

"I can meet you in a couple of hours. I need to talk to Tommy to find out what the hell is going on."

"Okay, I'm going to wear those lace panties that you like. You know, the ones that make my ass look extra fat."

"Hell yeah," JoJo said, though the only ass he was concerned with at that point was his own. He knew that if Manny started ratting, everybody would go to jail. Although Tommy was his childhood buddy, he didn't know how that shit would play out if Manny started a drug conspiracy. He hung up the phone and called Tommy, who answered the phone right away.

"Hey, I was just about to call you."

"Why? What's going on?" JoJo tried to act surprised. He couldn't let him know that he'd spoken to Nia.

"Bad news. Manny is in custody in Miami. His brother, Hector, called."

"Damn. So what does this mean? Are we finished or do we need to pack up our shit and get out of town or what?"

"No. Don't worry about that. Manny only knows me. He met Twin once, but I don't think nobody has anything to worry about. Manny ain't that type of guy."

"Tommy, you know what? Real estate don't sound like a bad idea after all."

"Now you see what I mean, huh?"

"I do."

"JoJo, rest assured, if Manny were to implicate me in anything, I would never do anything to hurt you. I love you like a brother."

JoJo was speechless. He hadn't expected Tommy to say that. Suddenly, he felt bad about sleeping with Nia. His friend was a good guy overall, and he was loyal, which was a rare trait nowadays. "Tommy, I love you, too."

*****

Nia stood in front of the bed, her hands down flat on the mattress. JoJo grabbed her small waist then pushed himself inside of her as deep as he could go.

"Damn, Daddy, not so rough!" she screamed.

"You said you wanted it, now shut up and take this dick."

"I like when you talk rough to me."

JoJo slapped her ass hard and pulled her hair.

"Pull my hair harder."

JoJo thought about Fatboy, and then he looked down at Nia the slut. The site of this good-for-nothing woman made him harder. He pulled her hair as hard as he could without yanking it out, and the slut was enjoying every minute of it.

They changed positions. She looked down at him, pressing his chest with her hands. The juices from her vagina drenched the condom, and the smell of sex lingered in the air. He still couldn't help but think about Tommy and how he'd said he loved him earlier. Still he was doing some foul shit.

Nia finally stopped moving. "What's wrong?"

"Nothing's wrong. I am just tired, that's all." He slid from underneath her.

"You're not into it."

JoJo got up and walked into the bathroom. He turned the water on, grabbed a towel, and began to wash his face.

Nia had followed him. "JoJo, what is going on with you, man?"

He turned and faced her. "I don't feel right fuckin you behind Tommy's back."

"Oh my God, this nigga gets a conscience now."

JoJo narrowed his eyes. "You know what Tommy told me today?"

"No, and I really don't care right now." She grabbed JoJo's arm and tried to pull him back to the bed, but he wouldn't move.

JoJo yanked his arm back. "I'm going to tell you anyway."

She stood silently.

"Tommy said he loved me like a brother. I believe that shit, too, man. Your man has a good heart, and this is the fuckin thanks he gets, a slut like you."

"Nigga, don't you go blaming me for this shit. First of all, Tommy has a problem that he won't correct. His dick won't get hard. Second, I never forced you to get with me. I didn't rape you. And third, that nigga, Mr. Innocent, came home last night with lipstick on his collar, so don't give me the bullshit."

JoJo stared at her for a brief moment then walked over and hugged her.

She gazed at him through teary eyes. "JoJo, I love Tommy, too. And I know he's a good person, but I have needs. Everybody has needs. Don't think that I enjoy fuckin around on him."

"I know you have needs, but this creeping around is really starting to get to me."

She shoved him away then got dressed, slipping her thongs inside her purse. She left without saying goodbye.

CHAPTER 10

"**I** need to meet with your daddy right away," Tommy said to Alicia.

"Tommy, what's wrong?"

"I would rather tell you in person."

"Is there something you can't say over the phone?"

Tommy hated when people asked that. He thought it was a no-brainer.

"Let's just meet somewhere."

"Like where?"

"Have you eaten yet?"

"No," she said.

"Let's meet at the *Cheesecake Factory*."

*****

The wait at the *Cheesecake Factory* was about an hour. Tommy didn't really care for the food there. He thought it was highly overrated. He thought it was just one of those places where the superficial went to be seen, just to say they were at the *Cheesecake Factory*. Since becoming a big drug dealer and making a lot of money, his life had become mostly artificial.

The hostess finally came and seated them in a booth in the front of the restaurant.

"So what's up, Tommy?" Alicia asked.

"The worst thing that could possibly happen."

She narrowed her eyes.

Tommy drank from his glass of water, still not saying anything.

She looked around. Nobody was paying any attention to their table. "Okay, Tommy, what the hell happened?"

"Well, Manny got busted."

"Who is that?"

"That's my connect; you know, the guy that I get my product from."

"Yeah, I know what a connect is. I'm not green, you know."

"I know. I keep forgetting."

She smiled but didn't say anything. Instead she reached for his hand and held it briefly.

"Alicia, I need a new life."

"So what are you saying, Tommy?"

"I'm saying you were right. I can't go on like this. I need to see your dad and get some advice on how to clean up my act."

"So you think Manny might snitch on you?"

"That's not what I'm saying at all. In fact, I don't think Manny will tell on me."

She sipped her water then smiled. "Tommy, I want to help you, whatever you need me to do to make sure every thing is okay with you. I don't want to see another black man sent away to prison."

He smiled and she grabbed his hand again.

"Tommy, I don't want to see you in trouble."

"Alicia, when can we go meet your pops?"

"We can leave Friday, if you want."

*****

Alicia and Tommy stepped off the plane in San Francisco. They walked hurriedly to baggage claims, where Alicia's father was waiting.

She ran and embraced him. "Daddy, I've missed you so much."

Tommy looked on in both admiration and envy. He had never had a relationship with his father, and his mother was long gone. Damn, he missed her.

Alicia's father shook Tommy's hand.

"Glad to meet you, Sir," Tommy said, trying to be respectful.

"I want you to kill that *Sir* shit right now. My name is Don, so call me Don. We're going to be on a first-name basis."

Damn, this man is cool, Tommy thought.

Outside, a blue and gray Maybach Benz with a driver awaited them. The driver put the luggage away.

Tommy and Alicia got in the backseat.

Don got in the front. His cell phone rang and he answered on the second ring.

"Why don't you act all stuck-up and shit?" Tommy asked Alicia.

She looked confused. "What kind of question is that? Why would you want me to act stuck-up?"

"I don't want you to act stuck-up. It's just that your daddy is obviously rolling, and you ain't wanting for anything. Most people with money act a certain way."

"I don't have money; this is his money. I'm just going to school trying to get mine, if you know what I mean."

Don turned to face Tommy.

"I love this car," Tommy said.

Don chuckled. "You don't own one?"

"Yeah, I wish," Tommy said.

"You ain't living until you own a Maybach."

"I went to the dealership once inquiring about one, but the salesman said they cost $384,000.

"That's about right," Don said.

"Now that's what I call rolling."

"That's what I call paying your dues."

Alicia reached over Tommy and adjusted his seat. She put it in recline mode.

Tommy lay back like he was in a bed. *Damn. This is the life.*

What was there not to like? And the fact that they weren't stuck-up snobs made it better.

"I got to make one stop then we can go get something to eat," Don said.

When they drove over the Bay Bridge into San Francisco, Don turned to Tommy and pointed at what appeared to be a prison. "Do you know what that place is?"

Tommy looked confused. "Looks like a prison of some sort."

"Yeah. That's Alcatraz."

"That's the reason I gave up your occupation."

"That place is closed now, isn't it?"

"Yeah, that place is, but there are more prisons that are open."

Tommy chuckled a little, not really knowing what to make of Don's comment.

"Let's go over to Pier 39," Don said.

Alicia turned to Tommy. "You can visit Alcatraz if you want to."

"No, thank you. I've visited enough prisons in my life." Tommy smiled.

"So you've been on the inside, huh?" Don asked.

"Not quite, but my dad is on the inside, and I go visit him quite often."

There was an awkward silence. Nobody wanted to say anything. Tommy figured the silence was because nobody wanted to offend him.

Finally, Don broke the silence and said, "Let's go get something to eat."

"Cool," Tommy said.

Five minutes later, they sat at *Dante's Seafood Grill*. A tall Asian woman walked up to the table.

Don rose to his feet and pulled a chair out for her.

"Tommy ... Alicia ... this is Jill, my new girlfriend."

Alicia shook Jill's hand then whispered in Tommy's ear. "Dad is a big womanizer, which is part of the reason he and Mom ain't together anymore."

"I thought they were together," Tommy said.

"No, they divorced last year."

Jill looked to be about twenty four. She was slim and attractive with big breasts.

Alicia and Jill made small talk about everything from makeup to handbags, while Tommy and Don talked about investing and making money.

"What kind of investing would you like to do?"

"Actually, I don't know. That's what I want you to school me on."

"I buy properties in neighborhoods where I anticipate the value will rise and then I sell them for profit. I started with residential, but made a transition into the commercial stuff."

"You seem to be doing well at it."

"I am. I have no complaints." He smiled then Jill gave him a kiss on his cheek.

"I want to live like you."

"Tommy, you haven't even seen the half yet. All you saw is the Benz. I got a Bentley. I have a home in the same neighborhood as Barry Bonds."

"Real estate helped you get all of that?"

Jill flashed a veneered smile. "Look at the bracelet Bunchy bought me," she said, showing a diamond-encrusted bracelet.

"Bunchy?" Alicia said then giggled.

Don smiled. "Yeah, we have pet names for each other."

"He calls me *Chinky* because of my eyes."

Tommy was still looking at the bracelet. It was flooded with diamonds. "That bracelet must have cost a grip?"

"Forty-five thousand dollars."

Damn, Tommy thought. He wanted to be able to drop forty-five thousand dollars on some jewelry and drive a Maybach Benz without worrying about the feds. "So what do I need to start making money?"

We'll, there's a high-rise building downtown; it's an office building I want to purchase. I'm looking for investors. Would you be interested?"

"Hell yeah. When do we start?"

"Okay, the building is going to cost us ten million dollars. I estimate in another year it will be worth twice that, or we can simply rent the office suites out and make half a million dollars a year. We'll probably be paying $250,000 in mortgages for the building, which means we'll clear $250,000 in profit."

Tommy's eyes lit up. "I'm ready."

"Slow down, man. You haven't even seen the plans yet."

The waitress appeared. She was a tall slim blonde woman.

"Give me the finest bottle of wine you got," Don ordered.

"Daddy, I want a martini. It's too early for wine. Maybe later me and Tommy might have a night cap," Alicia said. Then she put her legs over Tommy's. The return of the erection. Tommy smiled.

"Sir, would you like to run a tab?" the blonde asked.

Don pulled out a black American Express card.

"Now, see? That's why I don't need to see a business plan." Tommy pointed at the card. "I have no reason to doubt you, and I want to be a part of this."

Everybody at the tabled laughed.

"So, Don, how much is it going to cost to invest in the building?"

"Tommy, I'm going to need at least 1.5 million in cash."

Tommy took a deep breath. He tried to maintain his composure. At last count he had about four hundred thousand dollars. He'd hoped that he could do something with that. He thought about the fact that Manny was now in custody. He didn't know if he could even come up with that much money. He would be stuck in the drug game forever, the game that he so desperately wanted out of.

The waitress returned with wine and a martini.

Tommy finally said "Don, I don't have that kind of money."

"Daddy, that ain't fair. Can't you let him invest on a smaller scale?" Alicia suggested.

"Actually, I can. But he won't make as much money," Don said then smiled at Tommy. "See, guys like me and Tommy, we like the big bucks; a little won't do. Right, Tommy?"

Tommy put his hands around Alicia. "Your Dad is right. I want it all or nothing."

"So, how much can you invest?"

Tommy said, "I can have a million dollars in two months." He couldn't believe he'd actually said he could have that much money. He'd never made that much money before. He never believed he could make that kind of money, but he wanted the lifestyle Don was enjoying. But more than anything, he wanted to be able to say that he was legit.

Don shook Tommy's hand, and the deal was finalized.

*****

Tommy and Alicia checked into a hotel room in Pacifica, California. Alicia declined her Daddy's offer to stay in his home because he'd said that Tommy would have to stay in the guest room. She wanted Tommy to sleep with her, so they would have to get a room for themselves. The Best Western Hotel in Pacifica overlooked the Pacific Ocean. Alicia had gone there on her prom night. This is where she'd lost her virginity. Alicia showered first, then Tommy showered fifteen minutes later.

When Tommy came out of the bathroom, he discovered Alicia lying across his bed wearing only a white thong. He sat on the edge of the bed with his back toward her.

And she pulled him back and bit down on his neck. "I like you, Tommy."

He could smell the alcohol on her breath. He also noticed the condom packet in her left hand.

Alicia nibbled on his ear.

He gripped her ass then he started kissing her stomach. His statued penis demanded freedom from his silk boxers.

"Tommy, do you want to fuck me?"

"Hell yeah."

She then turned over in bed and got on all fours. The white thong contrasted beautifully with her skin. "Tommy, come and get this. It's all yours."

He slid two fingers by her thong and into her vagina.

"Yes, Tommy. That shit feels so good. Oh my God, that feels good."

He continued to stroke her vagina. His penis was damn near aching with each throb.

"You want this pussy?" she whispered.

"You know I want you."

She slid away from him, got up and walked toward the balcony door. "Tommy, have you ever fucked on a balcony?"

"Yes." He said, mesmerized by her long lean legs and her perfect ass.

"Overlooking the ocean?"

"No."

She signaled for him to come to the balcony.

Tommy walked to the balcony. Alicia stepped to him and pulled his boxers down.

The wind was blowing and the waves from the ocean pounded vehemently against the sea shore.

Alicia grabbed Tommy's penis and stroked it slowly. Then she dropped to her knees and massaged the head with her mouth.

After a few minutes of oral caressing, she stopped to fit a condom on his erection. Then she leaned over the banister. "Tommy, I need you inside me."

He entered her from behind and heard her moan. *Damn, this feels good.*

"Pull my hair, Tommy, and smack my ass."

Tommy obliged. He humped her hard and he could feel himself growing inside her. They changed positions. He pumped harder, pulled her hair, and smacked her ass.

"Talk dirty to me."

"You like this dick?"

"Yes, baby! Yes!"

When they'd banged out twenty minutes of balcony sex, they moved back into the hotel room. Tommy would get it up twice more over the next four hours.

CHAPTER 11

"**W**here in the hell have you been?" Nia asked Tommy.

"Handling some business," Tommy said, then walked into the kitchen and poured a glass of orange juice for himself.

Nia followed him. "Well you damn sure ain't been with JoJo and Twin, 'cause they been calling me for the past three days looking for you."

"I had to take care of something." Tommy gulped down the small glass of orange juice then refilled it.

"Oh, so we can't talk now, motherfucker."

Tommy took a seat at the kitchen table without looking up at Nia.

"Well, Tommy, are you going to talk to me, or are you going to keep playing these silly-ass games?"

He looked at Nia. He could tell she was genuinely upset. Perhaps she'd been worried, or perhaps she was angry because this time he left without telling her where he was going. He took a sip from the orange juice. "Nia, have you ever got a funny feeling that something bad was going to happen … and you just wanted to make preparations for it."

She sat across the table from him. "Tommy, what are you talking about?"

"I'm just trying to make preparations, just in case I get locked up, so I'll have something to fall back on."

"Tommy, don't talk like that."

"Well, it's the truth. I mean, it's a possibility."

"So what are you doing?"

"I met with a guy this weekend, and he's a real estate investor in California."

"Nigga, you've been to California and you couldn't tell me that you were going?"

"This was a business trip, not a personal trip."

"Still ... you didn't ask me if I wanted to go. Tommy, are you hiding something?"

Tommy didn't say anything. His mind drifted back to the hotel room with Alicia.

"Okay, Tommy. You ain't trying to answer me, huh?"

"I ain't got nothing to hide. I got the call from Manny's brother saying he was in trouble, so I had to get out of here to get my thoughts together."

She thought about his answer. "Legitimate now, huh?"

"That's the plan."

Nia walked over and put her arms around him. "That's good. Real good. I mean, I would hate for something to happen to you; you are such a nice guy. You know what I mean?"

He looked in her eyes. He couldn't believe she was concerned about him. He and Nia had had their problems in the past, but it was nice to hear that she thought he was a good person. "Nothing is going to happen to me because I am going to make money legitimately."

Tommy's cell phone rang. He answered on the second ring. "Hello."

"What's up, nigga?" It was Twin.

"Not much. Just got back from Cali."

"Oh, nigga, you just disappeared without telling nobody shit, huh?"

"I got a lot on my mind. I left so I could think."

"So are you still going to make this money or what, man? I'm hurting out here."

"Come over. Let's talk in person."

"I'll be there in five minutes."

*****

JoJo and Twin sat at the kitchen table. "So what's the word, Fatboy?"

Tommy's face was serious. "I've been thinking about this real estate thing hard, and I want to pursue it, man, before we all get locked up."

"Nigga, what makes you think we're going to get locked up?" Twin said.

"I don't know if were going to get locked up, but I know the outcome of these situations are usually ugly. I mean, look at Jamal and Dawg. Look at Prince and JB, Cornbread and Rollo ... These niggas are legends in the drug game, and they are all either in jail or dead."

"So you're quitting?" JoJo asked.

"No. I can't quit just yet. I'm going to need to get a million dollars before I can quit. A million dollars will set me straight."

Twin laughed. "Hell, if I could make a million dollars I would quit, too. Ain't no goal in the drug game. A million turns into two million, and two million turns into three, and three turns into the pen."

"Exactly. And that's what I'm going to avoid."

"So who is going to school you on the real estate game?" JoJo asked.

"This old cat named Don. This nigga is so rich, the nigga got a Maybach Benz and shit. He's made it in the game."

"So let me get this straight … You need to make a million dollars to give to this man to invest," JoJo said.

"Right."

"So what are you going to make off the money?"

"Like two hundred thousand dollars in a year, then we'll do more investments and make more money," Tommy said enthusiastically.

"That ain't no fuckin money," Twin said.

"So, *you got* two hundred thousand dollars?"

"No, but I look at it like this: Why spend a million to make two hundred thousand dollars?"

"Because it's legit."

"Fuck being legit," Twin said. "I'm going to be a crook for life."

"So, Tommy, what's up with Manny?"

"He's still in jail, but I'm going to call his brother and see what's going on. If we have to, we'll buy from his brother."

"Now that's what I'm talking about—doing what we do best," Twin said, smiling.

*****

Twin was in the drive-thru line at *Taco Bell* when a man walked up to the car and said, "Open the door, nigga."

Twin looked up and recognized the man. He smiled and opened the door.

J-Black sat on the passenger side of the Range Rover. "Order me a chalupa and a Sprite, nigga."

When they got to the window to pay, the bill came up to $8.93. Twin glanced at J-Black. He wanted to ask him for his portion of the money, but J-Black's expression looked as if he had no intention of paying.

Twin pulled away from the window. He handed J-Black the chalupa then the Sprite.

"I've been tailing you every since you left that faggot-ass nigga's house."

"Tommy?"

"Yeah, that motherfucker."

"So where's you car?" Twin asked.

A sudden hardness appeared on J-Black's face. "Don't worry about where my car is. That shit don't concern you."

Twin steered the car into the middle of the road then stopped at the traffic light. He added some mild sauce on his taco then pulled away from the light. They rode in silence.

Twin wondered what in the hell was on J-Black's mind.

"So what's been up with Tommy?" J-Black asked.

"I don't know," Twin said.

J-Black pulled out a chrome 9mm then cocked the hammer. "Wrong answer, muthafucka. I know you know what's up with him because you just left his house."

Twin pulled the car to the side of the rode. "J-J-J-Black, man, please put the gun away."

J-Black aimed the gun at Twin's head, took a bite of his chalupa then squeezed the trigger.

*****

Mark Pratt was at a table all by himself, in the Uptown Carousel, when Jennifer spotted him.

"Greetings, officer," she teased.

"Don't say that too loud."

"So who are you watching tonight?"

"I'm not watching anybody. I just thought I would come by to check you out."

"So you're in my fan club, huh?"

"I wouldn't say all that," Mark said as he examined Jennifer's evening gown. The gown was red and it gripped her body firmly. It was cut low at the top, revealing her huge breasts. Mark had never been a breast man; he'd always liked a woman's ass. Jennifer had breast and ass, and this was a rarity for a white woman. Though her breast were probably on a payment plan, they looked nice.

She sat on his lap. He could feel his erection forming. He thought about the last time he'd had sex.

She grabbed his face. "So, are you going to buy me a drink?"

"Sure, why not?"

Jennifer stopped the waitress and ordered a double shot of Hennessy and Coke. Mark asked for a water. Their drinks arrived less than a minute later.

Jennifer drank her Hennessy in three gulps, and then said, "You know, Pratt, you're not a bad looking guy."

"Thanks, Jennifer."

"How old are you?"

"Guess."

"Thirty?"

"Would you believe that I'm thirty-five?"

"No. You're kidding."

He pulled out his driver's license and handed it to her.

She stared at the picture for a long time.

"What are you looking at?"

"Scorpio, huh?" She smiled mischievously.

"What is that supposed to mean?"

"Means you're a freak, Pratt."

He took a drink of his water.

When the waitress came, Jennifer ordered another Hennessy and Coke.

"I'm a freak, huh?"

"Scorpio's are sexual beings. They love sex. I know because I'm a Scorpio.

"Oh, really?"

She licked the side of his face. His penis started bulging.

She grabbed it and winked. "Do you want me, Pratt?"

He was silent. God, he wanted this woman at least for tonight. He didn't answer her. Instead, he looked into her blue eyes; eyes that a lot of Blacks perceive as evil eyes. Black men had died for lusting after blue eyes and blonde hair, or at least speaking to them. The waitress dropped off a Hennessy refill.

Jennifer licked his face again.

"So, what do you see in Twin?"

"We're not here to talk about Twin, again, are we? Let's talk about me and you, Pratt. I know you want me, and I want you."

"Really? You think I want you?"

She held the glass of Hennessy up to his mouth.

He looked around. The music was amplified. A new Fifty Cent song played in the background. He opened his mouth slightly, and she poured the liquor down his throat. He thought about his dad, the good Reverend. What would he think of his son being in a titty bar with a stripper—a white stripper? He was playing with the devil. He was playing with Eve and he'd partaken of her forbidden fruit.

She kissed his jaw and grabbed his penis again, then she poured more liquor down his throat. "I want you, Agent Pratt, and I know you want me or else you wouldn't have come to the club tonight."

*****

Twin screamed, "Lord have Mercy, I'm dead!"

J-Black burst out with laughter. "Coward-ass nigga. Don't you know the difference between a blank gun and a real burner?"

"Quit playing like that, J-Black."

J-Black dug into his waistband, pulled out a black handgun, and cocked the hammer. "Now this is the real shit, nigga."

"Quit playing."

He took the clip out and showed twin the bullets. "Listen, mutha-fucka, I'm hungry out here, and I need to stick somebody. What about your boy? Do he have anything for me?"

"I don't think so, man. I mean, his connect is in jail. It's been kind of fucked up for everybody. What happened to the five bricks you kept?"

J-Black lit a cigarette. "Some muthafucka stole my truck that same day, with my stash in it, and I wasn't gone but two minutes in a store."

"J, man, this is my girl's truck. You can't smoke in here."

"I do whatever the fuck I feel like doing." J-Black blew rings of smoke at Twin's face. "Hey, I need a loan."

Twin dug into his wallet and handed him a one-hundred-dollar bill.

He snatched the money. "Don't fuckin play with me. This ain't no real money."

"I don't have no money, man. Didn't I tell you times was hard?"

"I know times is hard, muthafucka. Why do you think I'm out here fuckin with your punk ass in the first place?"

"Here is twenty dollars more," Twin said.

J-Black knocked the wallet out of his hand. "I need two thousand dollars, nigga."

"I ain't got that kind of money," Twin said.

"I guess your life ain't worth two thousand dollars, huh?"

"You wouldn't kill me; man, I'm your friend."

"I ain't got no friends."

"I got a thousand."

"That will do."

"I have to go home to get it."

"Let's go," J-Black said.

Twin thought long. He didn't particularly want J-Black to find out where he lived. "J, I can't take you to my house. My girl be tripping, man."

"So what am I supposed to do?"

"I can take you back to your car, if you want me to."

"Yeah. Take me back to my car. I want you to drive my car to your house; that way, I will know you're coming back. Understand me?"

Twin hesitated before speaking. "I guess so."

When they returned to Taco Bell, Twin jumped in J-Black's Impala.

*****

Twenty-five minutes later, Twin returned and met with J-Black, who was waiting in the car, smoking another Newport.

Twin handed him the money.

"Thanks, man. I appreciate this."

"No problem, J."

"Keep in touch. Make sure you let me know when old Tommy gets his hands on something again." He hopped out of the car and walked by the Impala.

"J, you're forgetting your keys."

"Nigga, those ain't my keys. I took the car from a coward-ass muthafucka in North Charlotte."

CHAPTER 12

Mark and Jennifer were lying on a bed in the Westin Hotel. He had made love to her twice already.

She lay in his arms, enjoying his company. "So how do you feel?"

He avoided her eyes and stared at the ceiling. "I don't know how I feel. I don't know what I'm supposed to say."

"Never had sex with a stripper, huh?"

"No."

"A white woman?"

"No. Never had sex with my informant, either."

"So this was a groundbreaking experience for you, huh, Pratt?"

"I wouldn't exactly put it like that."

"So, are you worried?"

"About what?"

She smiled. "That this will get out."

"No, I'm not worried about anything," he lied. He was concerned with what would happen if the agency found out that he crossed the line, and he thought about what his dad would say. This was not the type of woman he could bring home to Mama.

"So, did you enjoy it?" She rubbed his chest.

"I'm having a good time with you, Jennifer," he said.

"Good. I enjoyed it, Pratt. For a guy who's a square, you're a good lover."

"Is that so?"

"Yeah, but I knew it. You're a Scorpio."

"So what about Twin?"

"What about him?"

"Do you feel bad that you just had sex behind his back?"

She sat up on the edge of the bed. "Twin is fucking at least three different women other than me."

"What? That is dangerous."

"That's the life ... the drug life. It comes with the territory of being a drug dealer's girl."

"So why would you stay with him? Why would you stay with someone who cheats on you and obviously don't love you?"

Jennifer got out of bed and slipped on her jeans. Then she turned and faced Mark. "Like I told you before, Pratt, I have no choice. He is the only man that loves me—the only man that understands me."

"Twin is making money; he's making serious money, and he still lets you shake your ass in the club for me. I don't call that love."

Jennifer made eye contact with Mark, and then her eyes got misty.

Mark didn't like to see women cry. It did something to him to watch a woman cry. He sprang from the bed, walked over to Jennifer, and put his arm around her. "I'm sorry. I'm really sorry, Jennifer."

She jerked away from him. "Why are you being mean to me?"

Jennifer sounded like a child to him. He couldn't believe that she was that sensitive. He thought about what he said to her and he realized that he probably made her feel low. She'd made some poor decisions in her life, but she still deserved to be treated with respect.

She sat on the bed and started crying aloud.

"I apologize, Jennifer. I'm really sorry."

She looked up at him, mascara running and tears streaking her face. "You know what, Pratt? You've lived in a fucking bubble for most of your life. You don't know what it is not to have nobody in the world you can count on, do you?"

"I haven't had it good my whole life," Mark said.

"You ever go hungry?"

"Yes," he lied.

"Has your dad ever beat the shit out of your mom?"

"No."

"Ever been raped or molested?"

"No."

"I didn't think so, Pratt. You don't know the real world."

Mark sat beside her, grabbed her hand, and held it gently. "You're right, Jennifer. None of these things have happened to me, but I want you to know that you can make it."

"You think so, huh? What makes you think I can make it or, better yet, what makes you think that I ain't already making it?"

"I mean, there's a better life for you besides stripping."

"Like what? Witness Protection after you bring Twin and his boys down?"

"No, I didn't mean that, and I doubt if you're going to need witness protection from Twin. These guys are punks. Nobody is a gangster in that crew."

"What do you mean *there's a better life for me*, Agent Pratt? I don't have no education. What else can I do but take my clothes off for money?"

"You can go back to school."

"I don't have time to go back to school."

"Quit making excuses, dammit!"

"You're being mean again."

"Listen, I'm sorry, but I want to help you."

"Help me do what?"

"I want you to get away from this lifestyle."

Silence.

"Why do you want to help me?"

"I don't know… For some reason I want to help you."

"Do you like me, Pratt?"

He closed his eyes for a moment. Finally, he looked at her and said. "Far more than the law allows."

She laughed.

*****

At the *South Beach Marriot*, Twin, JoJo, and Tommy sat at a table in Tommy's suite. "So what's the deal with Manny's brother? Why hasn't he called you back?" Twin asked Tommy.

"I don't know, man. Your guess is just as good as mine."

"The muthafucka was telling us to come down, that everything was going to be okay. Now that we're down here, we can't get him to call you back. This is bad business," JoJo said.

"I agree," Tommy said. "I'll try to call him again." Tommy pulled out his cell phone and dialed the number.

No answer.

"Fuck this shit. Let's go on the beach. Let's go rent Ferraris and pick up some hoochies," JoJo said.

"We not here for that. We're here for business, remember?" Tommy said.

"Let's go get something to eat. At least by that time, hopefully, Manny's brother will have called you."

"Cool."

The Moon Room was crowded. Anna, the hostess, seated the crew at a table in the back of the restaurant. Twin and JoJo looked around at the beautiful Latina women who were walking around with pasties covering their nipples. "The shit is fuckin unreal," JoJo said.

"I feel like I'm in a fuckin movie," Twin said.

The waitress's name was Penelope. She was a petite woman with a nice, toned body. She approached the table with a bottle of champagne.

"We didn't order champagne." Tommy said.

"That's compliments of the gentleman up front." She pointed.

Their attention turned toward the man who had sent an eight-hundred-dollar bottle of Cristal to their table. He was alone at a small table.

Tommy asked Penelope, "Who is that guy?"

"His name is Juan."

"Tell him thanks for the champagne," Tommy said.

"I will," Penelope said, then passed out three menus. "I'll be back to take your orders." She sashayed away.

Juan approached the table. "My friends, whatever you want just let me know." He shook everybody's hand.

"You're Manny's friend, right?" Juan asked Tommy.

"Yeah. How'd you know?"

"I've seen you with Manny in the past."

"Really?" Tommy said, trying to remember Juan. But his face wasn't the slightest bit familiar.

"Manny's my cousin."

"We've been trying to locate his brother," Twin said.

Juan pulled up a chair. "So, you guy's in town for business or pleasure?"

Tommy was about to answer but JoJo nudged him.

"We don't know you," Twin said.

"Okay if I was the police, seeing your boy here with Manny a couple of weeks ago, all I would have had to do was follow him back to the hotel and hit the jackpot."

"Good point," Tommy said.

Juan smiled then got Penelope to bring him a rum and Coke.

"Listen. I want to make you guys millionaires."

Twin's eyebrows rose. "Really?"

Penelope interrupted, took their orders, picked up the menus, and sashayed off again.

"Yeah. Manny was cool, but he didn't give you enough room to grow."

"Manny did me good," Tommy said.

"Listen. I was Manny's supplier, so I know my price is cheaper than he could ever give you."

"You think so?"

"Did he give you kilos for ten thousand?"

Tommy didn't answer. He started to think about all the money he had at the hotel room.

"Ten thousand dollars?" Twin asked, surprised.

Juan sipped his drink then said, "Shhh. There may be undercovers in here."

"So when can we do this?" Twin asked excitedly.

"I don't think we should be doing this. I mean, Manny has always been my connect, and I've always went through him. I wouldn't feel loyal."

"Right answer," Juan said. "That's why every time you do business with me, I'll put something aside for him. Manny is my cousin, so you know my loyalty lies with him."

Tommy liked Manny, and he didn't want to seem like a business whore, but Juan was offering him the best price for coke.

Juan looked at Tommy. "So what's up, big man? Are we going to do business or what?"

"Juan, we're going to talk it over."

Juan stood and smiled. "Well, I'll be at the first table. You know where to find me," Juan said as he eased away.

Penelope came with more drinks. She said, "Eat as much as you want. Everything is on Juan."

When she left, they resumed their conversation. "We don't know this muthafucka, man," JoJo said.

"Hell, we didn't know Manny, either, the first time we met him," Tommy said.

"Tommy is right," Twin said.

"Man, do you know how much money we can make off this shit for ten thousand dollars a key?" Tommy said.

"Yeah. In the past, Manny would give them to you and you would sell them to us. Now we all have a chance of getting the coke directly from the source," Twin said.

Tommy hadn't thought about it that way. He'd always made money off JoJo and Twin because he was the one with the connection. Now they would be getting the product directly from the source as well. He didn't particularly like it, but he would deal with it because of the low price.

JoJo's eyes were squinted. He was contemplating.

"So, are we going to do it or not?" Twin asked.

"I just get a funny feeling about this whole situation," JoJo said.

"Nigga, our intention is to get rich, remember?"

"Exactly," Tommy said, remembering that he needed a million dollars fast. "I'm going to take a chance at it. Fuck it. It's only money."

"I ain't worried about the money part of it. I'm worried about going to jail, nigga. I hope you don't think that just 'cause the dude is Spanish that he won't arrest our ass. I mean, cops and informants come in all colors."

"I don't think he's a cop," Tommy said.

Twin looked at JoJo. "Come on, man. If Tommy don't think he's a snitch, it's gotta be safe, because that scary muthafucka thinks everybody is the police."

JoJo ate a forkful of salmon but didn't respond.

"So what is it? What y'all gonna do?" Tommy said.

"Lets go for it," JoJo said.

*****

Back at the hotel they counted their money. JoJo and Twin would spend thirty thousand dollars each. Tommy decided he would spend only a hundred thousand. He was being conservative, but he would profit the most out of the transaction. Their money covered the whole table.

*****

Juan frowned. "Man, I got sixteen bricks in here; you think we got time to bust all this shit open for you?"

"I'm spending a $160,000 here, too. I need to see them all."

Alex passed the bag to Tommy.

Tommy slit them all and took a minute to taste the product. Twin assisted him. "It's cool. It's all coke," Tommy said.

Alex smiled then collected the money. "Rather than count it, I will be the one to start our trust." He shook hands with the crew.

"We're going to do good business for a long time."

"Hell yeah, as long as the price stays sweet," Twin said.

"The price will only get better, my friend."

"That's what we want to hear," Tommy said.

CHAPTER 13

"**W**hat the fuck do you mean … *sheetrock*?" JoJo said angrily.

Tommy took a step back and pointed at the package on the table. "That's coke on top but inside it is sheetrock."

"I thought you tasted it, Tommy," JoJo said.

"I did, and Twin did too."

Twin silently paced the floor.

"Call that muthafuckin Juan right now. I ain't going out like that. I refuse to take an L," JoJo said.

"I know. I refuse to take a loss, too. Remember, I had a hundred thousand dollars invested," Tommy said. He pulled his cell phone out and dialed Juan's number. Nobody picked up. He tried three more times but got no answer.

"Nigga, you've caused me to loose thirty thousand dollars," JoJo said.

Tommy stared at JoJo, tempted to pull the small handgun that rested on his waistband. At that moment, he wanted to shoot JoJo in the face. He'd done so much for the man. He was the reason JoJo had money in the first place. Tommy had had the connection, and he'd always helped JoJo by providing him with coke. Now, he'd lost a hundred grand and JoJo had lost a measly thirty thousand dollars, yet Tommy was taking the blame.

"JoJo, you was in there looking at the coke, too, nigga. You can't blame Tommy. We are all in this together."

"Fuck that! He was the muthafucka who decided to deal with Juan in the first place."

"But nobody put a gun to your head and told you to deal with Juan."

"Nobody has put a gun to his head yet," Tommy said.

JoJo looked at Tommy. "What the fuck is that supposed to mean?"

Tommy pulled the small .380 from his waistband and put it up to

JoJo's temple. "Nigga, I will kill your punk ass."

Twin froze. He'd seen Tommy mad only a couple of times in his whole life, and he knew things could get ugly whenever he was mad. Fatboy was nobody's punk.

"So what are you going to do, blow my brains out Tommy?" JoJo said.

Tommy grabbed him by the throat, cutting off his wind. "I will kill you, nigga."

"So ... you wanna ... kill ... your boy 'cause you ... made a ... mistake."

"How? By helping you make money?" Tommy said.

"By picking up this bad shit." JoJo's pulse quickened and he looked faint.

"Let the nigga go, Tommy. He's going to pass out."

"Nigga, I made you into the man that you are today, and this is the thanks I get. Okay, you lost thirty thousand dollars, but it's because of me you got a nice place to stay, a couple of vehicles, and probably a small stash."

"You're right ... you're right, Tommy. Please ... let me go."

Tommy shoved him to the floor as hard as he could. He dialed Juan's number again. No answer. "I can't believe this shit!"

"I can't believe it, either, man. This shit is ridiculous," Twin said.

JoJo stood. He avoided eye contact with Tommy.

"So what do you think we should do?" Twin asked.

"Let's call Manny's brother and see what he knows about this shit."

Tommy called Hector.

Hector answered on the first ring. "Tommy, I'm glad you called. I lost my cell phone and I didn't have your number. Are you still in Miami?"

"No, I left yesterday."

"Sorry, man, for all the confusion."

"Yeah. I met a guy named Juan. He said he was Manny's cousin."

"Stay away from that guy. He's no good."

"It's too late. We've already dealt with him. He sold us sheetrock."

"Oh no. I'm sorry to hear that."

"Yeah, me too. We lost a hundred and sixty big ones in the deal."

"Come see me, Tommy. We'll make it up."

"I damn sure need it."

"Hey, listen, man. My brother told me to take care of you, and that's what I'm going to do. We will talk further when you get down here."

Tommy terminated the call.

"So what is Hector saying?" JoJo asked.

"He said that Juan is no good, and he is going to make it up to us."

"Cool. I feel a little better now."

Twin looked at Tommy. "So, basically, that guy Juan beat us out of our money, right?"

"That's what it seems like," Tommy said.

Silence. For a minute, Tommy thought about the hundred thousand dollars he'd lost. He thought about what he could have done with the money. He could have bought a house with the money, property that he would have had for years to come. Instead, he'd gambled the money away. "We're going to make it through this," he finally said.

"That's easy for you to say," JoJo said. "You still got plenty of money in your stash. I'm low, man."

Tommy extended his hand to JoJo. "What's mine is yours."

JoJo shook his hand, thinking of Nia. "And what's mine is yours."

*****

Jennifer showed up at Mark's office at 8:00 a.m. She looked very tired and exhausted. She had a black eye as if she'd been in a fight.

Mark smiled when he saw her.

She frowned and asked for some coffee.

"Decaff or caffeine, sweetie?"

"Give me the strong stuff … two sugars, no cream."

He left the office, made it to the lounge area, and made two cups of coffee.

When he returned, Jennifer had her head between her legs, crying.

"What's wrong?"

"Twin beat me last night."

"I was going to ask about your eye, but I didn't want to seem too nosey. So what did he hit your for?" He handed her the coffee.

"I don't know. He told me he'd lost thirty thousand dollars in some drug deal in Miami, and he just was kind of acting funny for the rest of the evening."

"And he hit you for that?"

Jennifer looked away. She stirred her coffee, only glancing at

Mark every once in a while.

Mark walked over and put his hand on her face. She looked up at him. She looked like a little girl, helpless and innocent. He no longer saw that rough exterior that came from her street experience. "Jennifer, why didn't you call the police?"

"I couldn't call the cops on him. He would kick me out, and I wouldn't have anywhere to go."

"You make your own money; you can get your own place."

She turned away. "You just don't understand."

"You love him, don't you?"

"Yes."

Mark walked to the other side of the office. He opened the blinds and looked outside, contemplating.

Jennifer stood and said, "I have to be going." She headed toward the door.

"Wait," Mark said.

She turned and faced him.

He looked at the bruises on her neck and face. He couldn't believe what had happened to Jennifer.

"So what are you going to do when Twin goes to jail? You know he's going. It's just a matter of time before we build a case strong enough to indict him."

Jennifer started crying. Her mascara ran, and she no longer looked like the glamorous beauty queen that kept all the men mesmerized.

Mark grabbed her face again. "Don't cry. Please don't cry. I hate to see you going through this."

She pulled away from him then wiped her face with her shirt.

"Jennifer, look at me. You can't go on like this. You have to get away from this guy."

"Are you going to help me out, Agent Pratt?"

"Yes, if I have to."

"Why do you want to help me?"

"I don't know. Why did you come to see me in the first place?"

"I guess I have feelings for you."

He leaned into her and kissed her briefly.

She put her hand around his waist and held him close.

The door opened and Ken Clarkson walked in.

*****

"Nia, I don't want to see you again. This shit ain't right," JoJo said.

"Since when did you start having a conscience, nigga?" Nia said. Then she walked into her bedroom with the cordless phone and lay across the bed wearing a T-shirt and a red thong.

"I just don't want to be caught up in the bullshit. I mean, I'm starting to get attached to you, and I don't want to betray my friend."

Nia laughed. "*Betray your friend*? We've been fucking for damn near a year, and you sure ain't had no problem before."

"I just don't feel like seeing you right now."

Nia rolled over in the bed. Now she was on her back. She put her hands between her legs. "Big Puss wants you, baby."

JoJo chuckled. "Girl, you're a nympho."

"Nigga, and you're a nympho."

"You're right. What kind of underwear do you have on?"

"I ain't got on no underwear. I'm naked, lying in my bed, stroking my pussy, and wanting you inside me." Nia laughed to herself.

"No underwear, huh?"

She burst out with laughter. "You freak, you know I got on underwear. I got on those red thongs you like."

"You got your heels on, too?"

"No, but I can put them on."

"Naw. I can't do it right now," JoJo said.

Nia sighed heavily. "So you're really going to cut me off, huh?"

"No. I'm not in the mood for it."

"Does it have anything to do with the money you lost?"

"How'd you find out about that shit?"

"Tommy's been moping around here crying and shit."

"Yeah, he lost a lot of money, a lot more than I did," JoJo said.

"Yeah he told me that you and him almost got into it."

"What did he say?"

"He said he put a gun to your head because you thought he was the reason y'all had lost the money."

"Oh, so he's bragging, huh?"

"Naw, he wasn't bragging. He was actually crying about it. He said that he'd never had an altercation with you. Said you was like his brother, and that he didn't like what went down between you two."

"See what I mean, Nia? Shit like that makes me not want to be screwing behind my friend's back."

"I know, but I got my needs, JoJo."

"I got my needs, too."

"Let's meet at the *Holiday Inn* downtown,"Nia said.

"How fast can you get there?" JoJo said.

She laughed. "Now that's what the fuck I'm talking about."

*****

Twin met with J-Black at *Burger King*. They sat in the back of the restaurant, in a booth. Nobody ordered food. J-Black had called and ordered Twin to either give him somebody to rob or become the next victim. J-Black had said he was desperate and needed money to pay probation fines.

"So what you got for me?"

"J, man, I don't have anybody. If I knew of somebody I would definitely tell you."

J-Black's eyes tightened. "Listen, Twin, I don't need to hear that bullshit, man. I need somebody to rob."

"I don't know of anybody. I'm telling you, man. If I knew of somebody I would tell you."

"What about that fat-ass nigga that I robbed the last time? How is he doing?"

"He's not doing too good, J. He lost a hundred grand."

J-Black stood and raised his shirt, revealing a chrome 9mm handgun. "Hey, nigga, I need somebody to rob, so we're going to your house so I can take all your shit."

Twin saw the seriousness in J-Black's eyes. The man had a reputation for being a killer in the street. He could think of only one other person worth robbing.

J-Black looked around. Nobody was looking. He pulled the gun from his waistband and aimed it at Twin. "Get the fuck up and let's get the hell out of here."

Twin stood and walked toward the door.

J-Black tucked the gun in his waistband and walked behind him.

Once they were in the parking lot, J-Black said, "You got somebody for me, or am I gonna have to take all your shit, nigga?"

"I got somebody for you, but I don't want you to hurt her. You know what I mean?"

"If she gives up the product, it won't be no problem."

"It ain't product. It's money."

"How much money?"

"Now that I don't know. But do me a favor … don't take it all."

"Now, would I do a thing like that?" J-Black said mischievously.

"Come on, J. Please don't take all of the money."

"Let's get in your car and you show me where the honey lives."

Twin drove J-Black to Melody's house. She lived in a small subdivision in the eastern part of town. Brawley Farms was the name of the community. Melody lived in a big two-story corner house, the front most property in the community. Twin pointed at the house.

"She ain't got no alarm, huh?" J-Black said.

"How do you know?" Twin asked.

"I don't see a sticker. I'm assuming. If she had an alarm, I'd have to do a home invasion and tie her ass up."

"That's good. I don't want you to hurt her."

"Muthafucka I ain't going in there while she's there, nigga. Don't worry about it."

"Good," Twin said. He hit the accelerator, quickly driving to the end of the street. They left the neighborhood.

"So where do you think the money is? Does the woman have a safe?"

"No. I never heard about a safe. I would bet the money is probably in one of the bedrooms."

"Good. This is going to be a piece of cake." J-Black smiled.

"Okay, I'm going to take you back to Burger King and you can handle your business from there, can't you?"

"I need a car … a getaway car."

Twin stared at J-Black. Twin definitely couldn't let him use his car to rob Melody. That was too risky.

"So, nigga, you going to let me hold the car or what?"

"Can't do that, J-Black."

"Why?" J-Black asked angrily.

He had to think of an excuse, something that J-Black would understand.

"Why can't you let me hold the car?"

"If my car is at the scene of the crime, somebody would suspect me."

"So? They wouldn't suspect *me*," J-Black said.

"But it's *okay* for them to suspect me?" Twin said.

"Come on, man. Let me hold the car. Nobody is going to see the car."

"Listen, J. If somebody sees the car, and they suspect me, then I won't be able to put you up on more robberies."

J-Black was silent for a moment. Finally he said, "Good point."

Chapter 14

The next morning, J-Black watched Melody from across the street. It was 7:00 a.m. when she put her five-year old son in the back seat of the back Honda station wagon and fastened his seatbelt. The car warmed up for about five minutes, and then she pulled off. When she was long gone, he went to the back door. It had four small glass panes. *This is going to be easier than I thought.* He rushed to his car and returned with a Phat Farm jacket wrapped around his right fist. He smashed out all four panes then tossed the jacket aside.

He opened the door and began to ransack the place. He searched the kitchen, the trashcans, the bathrooms, the hall closets ... but found no money.

Twin better not have lied to me, he thought. Finally, in the bedroom, he looked in the dresser drawers. Nothing. No sign of money. But he did find her underwear drawer. Thongs, bikinis, and G-strings. One of the G-strings had beads on it. *Damn. This is some sexy shit.* J-Black found a picture of her on the dresser. She was tall and light complexioned with long, wavy hair. *Damn, this one sexy-ass bitch.* He lay on her bed for a minute and imagined her with the beaded G-string on, strutting topless. He pulled out his penis for a minute and stroked it, and then he sniffed her underwear. He was on the verge of having an orgasm when he remembered what he'd come for.

He got up and headed for the walk-in closet. Melody had about fifty pairs of shoes. He started tossing all the shoes and boxes out onto the closet floor. Money spilled from two Jimmy Choo shoeboxes. J-Black's eyes lit up, thousands of dollars right there at his fingertip. He started to count the money but then decided that there was too much for him to count. He stuffed the bills back in the boxes, carried it all under one arm, and headed for the back door. He stopped and looked back at the G-string on the bed. He decided to get that, too.

*****

Later that night, at his run-down apartment, J-Black counted the money. He'd come up with thirty-eight thousand dollars. He smiled to himself. It had been a very good day, but not good enough. While his adrenaline was still going, he decided that Fatboy would be the perfect target again. He locked the place up and headed out to Lake Norman.

He arrived at Fatboy's house 45 minutes later and rang the bell.

A beautiful young lady answered the door. "Yes, can I help you?"

"Yeah, I was driving and I noticed that your car lights was on." He held a gym bag in one hand. There was nothing inside it but duct tape.

The woman looked puzzled. "My lights shouldn't be on. They should go off automatically."

"It's your interior light, sweetie." J-Black smiled. "I sometimes leave mine on unintentionally."

She stepped outside and closed the door. "Thanks a lot, sir." She walked toward the car before realizing the man must have made a mistake. "My lights aren't on," she told him.

He produced the 9mm. "No screaming. If you do, I promise I will shoot through your little sexy ass." He walked toward her and grabbed her arm. "Now take me back in the house and show me where the stash is."

She was too afraid to say a word. She led him back to the front door and opened it.

They were met by Tommy.

J-Black aimed his gun at Fatboy and smiled. "We meet again, muthafucka."

Tommy held his hands up. "Hey, man, I ain't got no fuckin dope."

"Where the fuck is the money, nigga?"

"I ain't got no money."

J-Black cocked the hammer of the gun. "You get over there beside him," he told Nia.

She quickly obliged.

"Where the fuck is the money?" J-Black asked again.

"I ain't got no money."

J-Black slapped Tommy with the butt of the gun and fired it at the same time.

Nia screamed.

Tommy fell to the floor and covered his face.

J-Black laughed. "Bitch-ass nigga. I didn't even shoot you. Get up off the floor before I pop one in your ass."

"Hey, listen. I think you should leave before the neighbors call the police."

"I don't give a fuck about the police."

"Tommy, give him the money," Nia said.

"I don't have no money here," Tommy said.

"Okay, muthafucka, this next shot will send you straight to heaven."

"I got some money in the dresser drawer," Nia said. "It's only a couple thousand dollars, though."

"I need that," J-Black said. "Stand up, man. We're going upstairs with your wife to get the money."

Tommy stood.

"Both of you go ahead of me. If you try any funny shit, I'll be the only one laughing when this gun goes off again."

Once they were in the bedroom, Nia searched frantically through the dresser drawers.

J-Black undressed Nia with his eyes. "Hey, sweetie, what kind of underwear do you wear?"

"Why?"

"You ever thought about doing lingerie modeling? I mean, you have the body for it."

"No, I never thought about it, but thanks."

"I bet you got thongs and all kinds of shit in your underwear drawer, don't you?"

Nia looked disgusted with his question.

"Let me see your underwear drawer."

"Hell no, nigga. Are you some kind of pervert or something?" Tommy asked.

J-Black turned the gun on Tommy. "Shut the fuck up."

Nia opened her underwear drawer and she held up a purple G-string.

"You want to model it for me?"

"Hell no!" Nia and Tommy said in unison.

J-Black pulled out the duct tape from his gym bag and bound Tommy's hands and feet. Then he taped his mouth. He turned to Nia and smiled, revealing his crooked teeth. "By the way, my name is Black. What is your name?"

"I'm Nia."

"So, are you going to model for me?" He stepped toward her.

She started crying. "I don't want to."

He put his arms around her shoulders. "Don't cry. I promise I ain't going to hurt you. Just put your purple thong on and walk around the room."

"Then will you leave us alone?"

Tommy lay still, batting his watery eyes. He looked as if he couldn't breath.

"I promise."

She pointed at Tommy. "He don't look like he can breathe."

J-Black went over to him and ripped a hole in the tape, allowing air to enter.

Nia took off her jeans and stood in white laced panties that gripped her ass perfectly.

J-Black took off his pants then sat on the bed, stroking himself.

"What are you doing?" Nia asked.

"Nothing. Don't worry about me; just walk across the room for me."

She walked across the room then turned around.

When he saw her ass jiggling, he said, "Goddayum."

"You're a sick man, Black."

"Put on the purple G-string and take off your shirt."

She obliged. Moments later, she was standing wearing nothing but the purple G-string.

"Put some heels on," J-Black ordered.

She went to her closet and slipped on some three-inch heels.

J-Black smiled then said, "Walk across the room."

She followed orders.

He began to stoke his erection again while grunting and making faces. He suddenly stopped for no apparent reason, then he walked over to the underwear drawer and picked out a little red teddy. "Put this on."

She put it on and walked for him again.

He walked over to her, naked from the waist down, penis

swinging stiffly, and touched her ass.

"No touching. You promised you wasn't going to do anything to me."

He laughed then said, "I'm sorry." He walked back to the underwear drawer and rambled through it until he found a black leather G-string. He was about to close the drawer when he noticed two light blue diamond-shaped pills. "What the hell are these?"

"Viagra."

"Whose is it?"

"It's nobody's."

"It's gotta be somebody's. It's in your drawer."

Nia took a deep breath then said, "I was going to give it to my boyfriend to try."

J-Black glanced at Tommy. "Nigga, your dick won't get hard for this fine-ass woman?"

"Come on, man, we don't have all day. What do you want me to do?" Nia asked.

"Put the leather G-string on and take that teddy off."

When Nia put the G-string on, J-Black returned to the bed and started stroking himself again. Then he suddenly got an idea. "Nia, why don't you bend over?"

"What?"

He cocked the hammer of the gun. "Bend over, I said, or I'mma put another hole in your ass."

She bent over. He began to stroke himself faster and faster until he was about to climax, but he stopped. "Do you have a condom?"

"No, I don't have any. Why?"

J-Black got up and walked over to the drawers. He couldn't find a condom. He pointed the gun at Nia and ordered her to get on the bed. When she got on the bed, he pointed the gun to her temple. "Now take the G-sting off."

"Please don't hurt me."

"Nobody is going to get hurt if you do what I say. Understand?"

Tommy squirmed on the floor.

J-Black turned. "I will blast you in the face if you move one more centimeter."

"Tommy, don't move. It's going to be okay."

"Take off your G-string."

Nia tossed the garment to the floor.

"I'm about to show you what to do with your woman's pussy, nigga. Since you're having a problem with your dick, I'mma fuck her real good."

Then he turned Nia on her stomach and entered her.

She moaned.

Tommy closed his eyes.

"Yeah, this is what the fuck I'm talking about. This is what you been missing, huh? That thug loving. I'mma give you that thug loving."

Nia began to cry. "Come on, hurry up."

"I'll finish when I finish; you know what I mean?" J-Black said. He looked back at Tommy, who still had his eyes closed. "No need to close your eyes now. It's real. I'm fucking your girl."

Tommy opened his eyes occasionally. Tears ran down the side of his face.

J-Black continued to hump long and hard. He couldn't reach an orgasm. The red teddy that Nia had modeled in was on the bed. He picked it up and started sniffing the crotch as he humped.

Forty-five seconds later he came. He hopped out of bed then put his boxers and pants on. "Bitch, give me the two thousand dollars you had ... and I'm gone."

Nia covered her face and cried.

"Give me the fucking money, I said."

She stood, went over to the dresser, dug in the bottom drawer, and gave him two thousand dollars.

After he'd ordered her to walk him to the front door, he left running.

There was no car in sight.

*****

"What the fuck do you mean somebody broke in your house?" JoJo asked his sister Melody.

"Somebody broke in my house; that's what I'm saying."

"Did you call the police?"

"No, not yet. I just discovered it when I got home."

"I'm coming over." He terminated the call in her ear then called Tommy.

"Hello."

"Somebody broke in my sister's house," JoJo said.

"And ... the same dude that robbed me the first time came back and robbed us again; but this time he tied me up and sexed Nia. We're on our way to the hospital so they can get his DNA sample."

"Something is strange. This sounds like an inside job; you know what I mean?"

"I know what you mean, Jo. Have you called Twin to tell him what is going on?"

"No, not yet, but I'm going to call the nigga in a minute. Now I'm on my way to Melody's house to see what's going on."

"Call me when you get there."

"Okay," JoJo said. Then he asked, "Is Nia okay?"

"She's all right. Still kind of shook up from the whole incident."

"I can imagine."

*****

When JoJo got to Melody's house, he ran and hugged his sister and her little son Tyree. "You okay, Sis?"

"Yeah, I'm okay. We weren't here ... thank God. I don't know what I would have done if we were here."

"I would have beat him up, Uncle JoJo."

JoJo smiled at his nephew. Then he thought about what might have happened had his sister been home. He and his sister were very close. It was just the two of them; their mother was in a mental institution. He didn't know if he would be able to handle it if something were to happen to her. "Did he take anything?"

Melody looked at her brother then turned her head briefly before resuming eye contact. "Yes. He took the money."

"You're kidding me, right?"

"No, JoJo. I had the money in a couple of Jimmy Choo shoeboxes. When I looked for it, it was gone."

"That's just fuckin great, Melody. That shit really makes my day."

Melody covered Tyree's ears then ordered him to go to his room. When the child was gone, she said, "So that's all you care about is your damn money, JoJo?"

JoJo looked at his sister; tears had formed in her eyes. He stepped forward and hugged her. "You know that ain't true. It's just that I lost some money last week. All of this came at a bad time."

"JoJo, I'm sorry."

JoJo kissed his sister's forehead. "Don't worry, baby girl, it's going to be okay."

"Come here and let me show you the broken window."

JoJo followed his sister to the back door. Glass was still on the floor. He walked outside and discovered a jacket on the back deck. "Look, Melody. Look what I found."

"A jacket. The man must have left his jacket. Check inside the pocket and see if there's anything else that we can use as clues."

JoJo dug into the pockets and found four business cards and some keys.

Robert's Used Appliances.
Robert A. Moray
Home # 704-555-2345
Cell # 704-555-8976

JoJo handed the cards to his sister. "Call the number on the card."

Melody obliged. She called his home number first and got an answering machine. Then she dialed his cell phone number and nobody answered the phone.

CHAPTER 15

Mark Pratt and Ken Clarkson had coffee at a Starbucks around the corner from the office. This was the first time they had been together since Ken had walked in on Mark and Jennifer as they hugged. "So what's going on with you and the girl?"

"What are you talking about?" Mark said.

"You know, the stripper chick."

"Nothing is going on with her."

Ken raised his eyebrow. "Are you sure?"

Mark avoided his eyes. "Yes, I'm sure."

"Either you like her or she likes you."

Mark sipped his coffee slowly. "Why do you say that?"

"I just got a gut feeling that something ain't right."

"What are you trying to say, Ken?"

"I hope I'm wrong about this. I mean, the girl is dirt and she's a drug dealer's whore. You don't wanna have anything to do with someone like that, do you?"

The words *drug dealer's whore* echoed in Mark's ears.

"You need to be careful what you say about people."

"I'm just saying, if you are fuckin with that girl, you're in dangerous territory. I mean, I hope I'm wrong. This woman is a sleazy character, and all I'm saying is you don't need to be involved with someone like that."

"I'm not involved with anybody."

Ken looked at Mark with serious eyes. "How old are you now?"

"Thirty-five."

"And you aren't married? What's the problem?"

"I don't know. I'm just waiting on God to send the right woman in my direction."

"You're almost forty."

"Your point is?"

"I don't have a point. I just know that marriage brings stability in your life."

Mark looked confused. "Are you trying to say I'm unstable?"

"Just saying there's a lot of temptation out there for a single man."

"You have the same temptation that I have."

"But I have my vows with my wife to keep me focused."

"Well, I have Jesus."

"Jerry Falwell, Jim Baker, and Jesse Jackson all had Jesus, too. Look where it got them."

"What are you saying?"

Ken took a deep breath. "Just stay away from that woman."

*****

At Twin's downtown condo, JoJo, Tommy, Twin, and Jennifer sat at the kitchen table.

"The nigga left a jacket at my sister's house," JoJo said.

"Where is the jacket?" Twin asked.

"The police got the jacket."

"You went to the cops?" Twin asked.

"It was my sister's idea to go to the cops, especially when I told her what happened to Nia. She just didn't feel safe no more."

"Does your sister live alone?" Jennifer asked.

"Yeah."

"I think you should let her move in with you for a while, at least until they apprehend that creep," Jennifer said.

Twin read the card aloud. "Robert A. Moray."

"The nigga that broke in my house said his name was Black."

Twin gave JoJo the card.

"He told you his name?" JoJo asked.

"Yes. Well … he told Nia his name."

"Where were you when he raped Nia?" Jennifer asked.

"Tied up. He made me watch."

"He needs to be brought to justice. This is the kind of person that needs a life sentence," Jennifer said.

"Well, the police took a report and the hospital swabbed his semen sample from her."

"So, how is Nia doing?" Jennifer asked. "I feel really bad for her, even though I've never met her."

"She's doing better," Tommy said.

"So, are you sure that he is the guy that robbed you before?" JoJo asked.

"Yeah, the same nigga. He is one bold muthafucka."

"I think the two robberies are related," Jennifer said.

"Naw, I don't think so," Twin said.

"Shit. Sounds like they are," JoJo said.

"If that's the case that means it would have to be an inside job, and I know nobody in this room would be cold enough to set up no robberies," Jennifer said.

"Shit just don't seem right to me," Tommy said.

"It's an inside job," Jennifer said.

Twin turned to face her. She was making him sick with her analysis of the situation. Now she had his friends wondering and considering an insider. He pointed toward the living room. "Jennifer, get the fuck out of here and let me and my friends talk."

She looked at him and started to protest but didn't. She just left the room with her head down.

"So what are we going to do now?" JoJo asked.

"Find the muthafucka that has done this shit and have him knocked off," Twin said.

"That shit is easy to say, but we don't have no way of finding this man."

"Shit, you're the one who said you saw his face. I can't believe you talking all this stupid shit," Twin said.

"Yeah, I saw his face. But what am I going to do? Go all over Charlotte looking for him?"

"No, but we can call the muthafucka on the card," JoJo said.

"Call him then," Tommy said.

JoJo pulled out the card then dialed the number. A voice recording came on. "No answer."

"Okay, we've been robbed, but we got to make this money. I got real estate that I want to buy. I got to get out of this business. I ain't trying to go to prison."

JoJo stared at Tommy long and hard. "I understand where you're coming from, but understand this: We just lost money in Miami and now this coward done robbed both of us. We can't let people think we're pussies, and that they are going to just take from us."

"I'm with JoJo. Ain't nobody gonna take shit else from me. I will die for mine," Twin said.

"I feel ya, but if we go out and find ... Black, kill him, and catch a murder case, we ain't going to be able to do shit."

JoJo sighed aloud. "I didn't think about it like that, but I guess you're right. What am I supposed to do? I ain't got no money, man. This shit has sunk my fuckin battle ship."

"I done told you, what I have is yours. Manny's brother wants me to come talk to him; let's try to get down there."

"Let's drive then, 'cause I don't want to go through any of that shit like getting harassed at the airport," Twin said.

"In the meantime, I'm still going to keep trying this Robert Moray character."

*****

JoJo was lying across the bed. He began to wonder about Nia. He wondered if she was okay. He hadn't spoken to her since she'd been raped. He dialed her cell phone number.

She picked up after three rings.

"Hey, baby, can you talk?"

"Yeah. I'm at my mama's house, but I'm feeling kind of tired, you know?"

"I didn't rest easy when I learned you got raped."

"Ahh, that's so sweet."

"So how do you feel?"

"I feel kind of used up and dirty, and I've been having nightmares of him."

"Yeah, I know it must be tough for you."

"Trying to get adjusted. You know what I mean?"

"I want to see you. I miss you." He sat up in bed now.

"You miss me? Really?"

"Why do you sound surprised? You know I miss you."

"I know I miss *you* sometimes, and I've often wondered whether you ever miss me, or did you ever think about me."

"Well, now you know I miss you."

"I don't really want to be seen by nobody. I told you ... I feel so dirty, so undeserving of any attention."

"You need to stop talking like that. You are not dirty. The muthafucka that raped you has the fuckin problem, not you."

"I know. But that doesn't make me feel less contaminated."

"Contaminated? Don't be so hard on yourself."

"You missed me, huh?"

"You know this."

"What did you miss about me?"

"I missed being able to talk to you."

"Why did it take you so long to call?"

"I don't know. I was thinking that you and Tommy was spending a lot of time together."

"No, not really. He went to the hospital with me, but other than that, I've been here with Mama. I didn't want to stay at home. I don't feel safe no more."

"Yeah, I feel ya."

"You want to come over?" She asked.

"Yeah. I think it will ease my mind a bit if I saw you."

"You got me blushing."

*****

Tommy was at the lake when Alicia called. He'd only been navigating his boat, enjoying the weather. The sun was out, and there was a gentle breeze blowing.

"What you doing?"

"At the lake."

"Fishing?"

"Not yet. I'm just enjoying the weather."

"You coming to see me today?"

"I was going to ask you the same thing."

"I can come out to the lake, but I don't want to get on the boat. I'm scared we'll fall in, and I can't swim."

"You can't swim and you're from California?"

"What is that supposed to mean? Everybody in California don't know how to swim."

"I thought Cali was all fun and beaches."

"Wrong."

"Obviously I am." He laughed.

"Why don't you come over here and serve me, Big Papa?"

"You want me to come over now?"

"Unless…"

"Unless what?"
"Being on your boat is more important than I am."
"No, not at all. In fact, I'll be on my way in about thirty minutes."

CHAPTER 16

Alicia opened the door, wearing tight jeans, a tank top, but no shoes. Tommy smiled at her and she invited him into the living room. "Oh, yeah ... before I forget ... Daddy called me this morning, and he was wondering what's going on with you?"

"I had a setback, but I'll have the money real soon."

She frowned. "You had a setback? What happened?"

"I lost a hundred thousand dollars in Miami," he said. He wanted to tell her about the robbery, but that would mean he would have to tell her about the rape. Where Alicia was concerned, he was supposed to be a single man.

"You lost a hundred thousand dollars?"

"Yeah."

"Wow. I don't know what I would do if I lost that kind of money."

"I tell you what, it ain't easy. I've did all my crying, now it's time to go back to work."

"Get back to work? You are so much like my daddy."

"That's a good thing, ain't it?"

"It is in a way, but I'm not all about material stuff. I just want to be happy; besides, I'm going to school so I can provide for myself."

"So you don't care if I had money or not?"

"As long as you're able to take care of yourself, I could care less."

He smiled. "So you like Big Daddy?"

"Yes."

"You love me?"

She laughed then toyed with her hair. "You're pushing it."

"I've got you a gift."

"What is it? I love surprises."

"It's in the car. It will have to wait until I leave."

"Now you got me curious. I'm going to be wondering about the gift the whole time." She stood and walked past him seductively then closed the living room blinds.

He looked at her ass and remembered the sex they'd had in San Francisco. He wanted her again at that moment.

She turned and laughed.

"What's so funny?"

"I saw you staring at my ass. Men's intentions are so obvious."

"What do you think my intentions are?"

"You probably want some ass, since I put it on you in California."

"Am I that easy to read?"

"Come on; lust is written all over your face."

"So what are we going to do about that?"

"Nothing."

"So you're going to let me suffer like that?"

"I don't have a choice. It's that time of the month."

"Period, huh?"

She walked over, sat on his lap, and kissed him on the jaw.

"I think I'm falling for you," he said.

"That's a good thing, ain't it?"

"Yeah." He put his hand on her ass.

She slapped his hand. "Stop it."

"What did you do that for?"

"I don't want to get nothing started that I know we can't finish."

He kissed the back of her neck.

"Stop it, Tommy."

"Okay, I'm going to be a good boy now."

She looked him in the eyes. "Tommy, why haven't you ever invited me to your house?"

"I don't know. It just never came up, that's all. It's not like I'm hiding anything."

"Nobody said you were hiding anything, but since you said that ... are you hiding something ... like a family or something?"

"No. Hell no."

"So when you gonna take me to you house?"

"Anytime you want to go."

"Why not today?"

"I have to ... get ready to go out of town tomorrow. I have a flight to catch."

"But if I'd given you some ass, you would have had sex with me in a heartbeat."

114

"Would have been ready to fuck you on the spot." He smiled.

"Tommy, don't say that. Say have *sex* or make love. I'm a lady."

Tommy didn't say anything. Instead, he looked like a kid being chastised by his mother.

"Tommy, I want to go to your house."

"I can't take you today, maybe when I get back from Miami."

She looked at him suspiciously. "Tommy, you're not living a double life, are you? I mean, you don't have a family that I don't know about, do you?"

"No. What makes you say that?"

"Just curious."

Tommy stood and walked toward the door. "Come on outside. I got something for you."

"What is it?"

He smiled. "Just follow me."

When they arrived at Tommy's pickup truck, he grabbed a fishing pole from the back of the truck … a pink one, just like he'd promised. He'd actually painted it for her.

She burst out laughing. "Boy, you are too sweet."

"You like it?"

"Yes, thank you. But now I have to get me a cute little outfit to wear with you when we go fishing."

"Oh my God, woman."

She leaned toward him and gave him a kiss. "I still can't wait to visit your house."

*****

Hector Gomez wore slacks, a *Lacoste* shirt and expensive loafers. He met Tommy in the lobby of the hotel. They walked into the lounge area and took a seat at a table in the corner.

Hector ordered two bottled waters. "I'm sorry about what happened with Juan. I hate that you guys lost your money like that."

"So what can we do to make up our money? I know you're sorry, but that's not going to bring the money back."

"I know, but I can't give you your money back because I didn't have anything to do with it."

Tommy looked frustrated. He didn't respond. Instead, he thought about Manny and how they'd always done good business. His mind recalled Alicia's father and the real estate proposition.

"Listen, Tommy, the only thing that I can really offer you is product."

"How much am I worth?"

"I don't know, maybe ten kilos."

"Manny will tell you that I am worth a lot more."

"I know you are, but things have gotten pretty rough since Manny got locked up."

"You said you would make it up to us. Now how are you going to dot that?"

Hector sipped his water. "Have you ever sold pills?"

"What kind of pills? You mean like X?"

"Yeah." Hector smiled.

"I ain't never sold X. I've always been a coke man."

"Listen, there is plenty of money in X. I mean, you can make millions in months."

"Explain how."

Hector looked around to make sure no one was listening. The lounge area was pretty empty, except for a an elderly white couple sitting at the bar, telling the bar tender boring stories about when they'd lived in Toronto.

"Okay. I can wholesale you the pills for four dollars each if you buy at least twenty-thousand dollars worth, and you can wholesale them to your friends for eight dollars. They go for twenty in the streets. The money will come so fast it will make your head hurt; trust me."

"Twenty thousand dollars worth of pills … how in the hell will I get rid of those?"

"Man, believe me, it will not be a problem. Everybody takes pills. Everybody wants to feel ecstasy."

"So when can we get the product?" Tommy asked, anxious to start his new venture.

"Whenever you come back with the money."

"I got money now for the coke, but I didn't bring money for the pills," Tommy said. He had brought another hundred thousand dollars; and Twin had brought fifty thousand. "So front me the pills."

"If I give you the X on consignment, I will need five per pill."

"Cool."

"Okay. I'll go get the product, and we'll meet in the lobby of the hotel in an hour."

*****

"Nigga, that's a smart move. Everybody is doing X."

"That's what I've heard," Tommy said.

"How much are we going to get?" JoJo asked.

"About twenty thousand worth at five dollars a pill for me. I'll give them to you and Twin for seven."

"Cool. I'm with this. I can just get my girl to holler at the girls at the club and get them to get the word out," Twin said.

"I think we should wholesale the shit at maybe ten dollars a pill, then come back for more," JoJo said.

"That's what I'm going to do," Tommy said.

"You know somebody that would buy it wholesale?" Twin asked.

"I'll call my boy, Big Red, on the south side. That's all he fucks with," JoJo said.

"Just wait til we get back and go holler at him," Tommy said.

*****

Hector brought a clear Ziploc bag full of X to Tommy's hotel room. He dumped the pills onto the table. There were green ones, yellow ones, and pink ones. They had designs on them such as butterflies and Nike Swooshes. Some even had the Mercedes Benz symbol.

"Which ones are in the highest demand?" Tommy asked.

"They all are, but the Nikes are popular here in Miami."

"Nikes, huh?" Tommy thought about the whole concept of the pills. It was sheer genius. Someone had thought of putting these designs on the pills, branding the drugs, so the customers would recognize the product. Now his goal would have to be to make one of the designs his brand. The Nikes looked cool, but the ones with the Mercedes symbol would probably be better for a town like Charlotte. He wanted to sell his customers a dream. He wanted to sell them pleasure and sheer ecstasy.

"Okay, I'll take them."

Hector grabbed a handful of pills then put them back in the bag. "You'll see, Tommy. I'm going to make you a multimillionaire."

"So how come Manny never gave me a chance to sell X?"

"See, Tommy, we're kind of like a Syndicate. Manny does the coke; I'm into the pills and my father sells the heroin, but it all goes to the same family. And the reason why we are so strong is because we are family and nobody is greedy."

Tommy and Hector counted $150,000 for the coke; the pills were consigned, and the deal was confirmed with a handshake. Tommy promised to pay Hector back in two weeks ... even if the pills weren't sold.

*****

"Big Red wants to buy all the pills we have," JoJo said.

"How do he know what we got?" Tommy asked. "You shouldn't have called him yet."

"I told him that we should have about twenty thousand pills."

"How much he wants to pay?"

"Nine dollars a pill."

"I don't want to sell them," Tommy said.

"What? Nigga, are you crazy?" Twin said.

"No. I got a plan, one that's going to make us rich."

"Let's hear it."

"I want to retail this shit for fourteen dollars a pill. We want to pick the pill that gives the most pleasure then sell it for less than twenty dollars. And we'll set up pill houses."

"Pill houses?" Twin asked.

"You know, a place where customers can get their supply."

"I think I see where you're going with this," JoJo said.

Tommy was in deep thought. He knew that if he could implement his plan successfully, he would have the million dollars soon.

"What about the coke?" Twin asked.

"We are going to do both. We're going to have what everybody wants," Tommy said.

"Okay, who's going to take this shit back to North Carolina?" JoJo asked.

"Shit. I'll drive the coke back myself," Tommy said.

"What about the pills?" Twin asked.

"Shit. One of y'all drive that shit back," Tommy said.

"I can get my girl to come down. She can fly back with the pills."

JoJo stared at Twin. "Are you sure about that? I mean, none of us know how much time pills carry."

"Yeah, you're right, but I know I ain't going to take the shit back along with the coke," Tommy said.

"Fuck it. I'm calling my girl. We can put this shit in balloons and get her and one of her girlfriends to carry. I mean, who would ever suspect two white bitches?"

"Man, your girl has already been approached by the feds. What do you mean *who would ever suspect her*? She's already suspected," JoJo said.

"But what else can we do?"

"Let's let his girl do this just one time," Tommy said.

"Okay, just this one time. But we gotta do something else after this," JoJo said.

CHAPTER 17

Twin picked Jennifer up at the Miami International Airport. Her friend was Morgan, a tall blonde from Connecticut. Jennifer had met Morgan at the club about two years ago. The two girls had connected immediately. They had a lot in common. They both were voluptuous blondes, and both had grown up poor, with alcoholic parents, and they both loved men with money.

Once they were in Twin's hotel room, he explained the mission to them. He told them that they would be compensated greatly for their services.

"What do you consider *compensated greatly*?" Morgan asked.

"Two thousand dollars each."

Morgan nodded her head "Yes, this would be worth my time."

"So are you with it?" Twin asked.

"Yes, but I have one more question: How are we going to conceal the drugs?"

"Twin pulled out a pack of black balloons. "You stuff the pills in here and then swallow them."

"I don't understand. If I swallow them, how are you going to get them?"

Twin looked at Morgan. "You really are a fuckin blonde, aren't you? If you swallow them the only way it's going to come out is if you shit, right?"

"How disgusting," Morgan said.

"That's business. Now, are you with it or not?"

"Yeah, I'm with it, but how many pills do you have?"

"About twenty thousand pills."

"Twenty thousand pills? Are you fuckin stupid? There is no way that two of us can swallow that many pills."

Twin was silent for a moment. "We'll just have to … get you a rental car and you drive them back."

"That's twelve hours."

"And?"

"I'm going to need at least two hundred dollars more," Morgan said.

"You know what? You're one greedy-ass bitch," Twin said.

"That's my price. Take it or leave it."

"I ain't got know choice but to take it. But as soon as I can get somebody else to do this shit, your ass is out."

"Whatever," Morgan said.

"Let's go to Hertz to get the car," Twin said.

*****

A little more than a week later, Tommy and his friends were in Miami again. It was ladies night at Club Sky, and the line was comprised mostly of women taking full advantage of the opportunity. Tommy pulled up to the club and waved for Kenny, the huge bouncer, to come closer.

"Hey, Tommy. What's up?"

"Not much. Just wanted to park my car in front of the club."

Kenny placed his hand underneath his chin as if he were in deep thought. "You know, Tommy, I don't know if I can let you do that or not."

Tommy pulled out a roll of money and peeled off a couple of hundred dollar bills. "I need you to watch the car while I'm in the club."

Kenny stuffed the money in his pockets. "I gotcha, Tommy, and I'll get you and the boys in the club free. You can cut the line."

Tommy handed Kenny the keys. "If you need to move the car, move it, but come get me soon as you move. I don't need nobody breaking into my car to steal my shit."

"I gotcha, big man," Kenny said.

Inside the club Tommy, Twin, and JoJo went straight to VIP. Tommy ordered two bottles of Cristal. When the bottles arrived, so did the girls. There were tall ones, short ones, thin ones, thick ones ... They all wanted to know the big man buying the expensive champagne.

Twin looked at the girls with a disgusted look then whispered to JoJo, "Thirsty bitches."

Big Red, the ecstasy dealer from the south side, walked up to

JoJo. "What's up, nigga?"

"Nothing much."

"Hey, man, I need some of those butterflies."

"We ain't selling the butterflies."

"Why not?"

"Cuz, that's how we make our money."

"Listen, man, everybody wants the butterflies, and you give me this dolphin bullshit."

"I can't help you, man."

"I will give you twelve dollars a pill, but I want twenty thousand pills."

"You got $240,000?"

"Listen, I got it, man. I just need the product."

JoJo pulled Tommy to the side. "Hey, that's my nigga, Big Red, right there. He wants twenty thousand butterflies."

"He got the money for them?"

"Yeah. He even said he would pay twelve dollars a pill."

Tommy figured the profit in his head. "When does he need them?"

"Now."

"Well, you know we don't have them now, but we can get them in a couple of days for him."

"Cool. I'll tell him." JoJo stepped over to Red. "Hey, I can get the pills to you by Wednesday."

"That's cool," Red said. "I'll buy the next two bottles of champagne."

*****

JoJo called Robert A. Moray, the name on the business card. The robbery had been on his mind ever since it had occurred. Some guy answered the phone on the first ring.

"Hey. Good morning to you, sir. I'm JoJo."

"Good morning. How can I help you?"

"Just wondering if I could come by your place of business to look at some appliances."

"I don't work like that. You tell me what you want, and I can bring it by your house for you to look at."

"Why can't I come by your spot to look at what I'm buying?"

"Either we do business my way or no way," Moray said.

"Okay, I need a washer and dryer."

"You want the washer-dryer combination or you want them separate?"

"The combination."

"Okay, where do you live?"

"I live downtown at the Summit Grandview Apartments."

"On Morehead?"

"Yeah."

Moray took a deep breath. "That's a long way from me. Can we meet somewhere closer?"

"Where are you coming from?"

"Pine Valley."

"Okay, let's meet at the car wash on Clanton Road."

"That's still kinda far, but I guess I can make it there."

"How long will it take you?"

"I can be there in thirty minutes," Moray said.

"See you in thirty."

JoJo grabbed his .45 from the bedroom closest then loaded it.

*****

Moray was there already, in a white commercial van that advertised Moray's Used Appliances. He was sitting on the bumper of the van when JoJo pulled up. He looked to be in his fifties. His hair was peppered with gray, braided, and slightly thinning at the top. He was wearing a white T-shirt. His arms were covered with tattoos and he was smoking a Newport.

"JoJo?" he asked.

"Yeah."

"I'm Robert." He extended his hand.

JoJo shook his hand, and then he examined Robert.

"The washer and dryer is on the back of the van."

"Okay, first I have to call my wife. I want her to come and look at it."

"What kind of bullshit is this?" Moray said. He puffed his Newport. "Hell, if I had known this, I wouldn't have even came here."

"Calm down, man. I have to do this if I'm going to spend money with you."

"Man, this ain't no house you buying; this is just a funky-ass washer and dryer, and you gotta consult your wife?"

JoJo didn't say anything; he just ducked into his car, called

Tommy and Twin, and told them to come to the carwash.

Moray was on his third Newport when the Yukon Denali pulled up. "What the hell is going on here, man? You ain't trying to rob me, are you?"

"Calm down, Mr. Moray."

"Calm down? What the hell is going on? You tell me that your wife is coming; the next thing I know, you have your fucking crew come up here." Moray threw his cigarette down but lit another one.

Tommy and Twin walked up to Robert.

JoJo introduced them. "These are my friends, Tommy and Twin.

Moray squinted his eyes. "Why are they here?"

"Well, you see, Robert, there has been a robbery."

"What the fuck does that have to do with me?"

JoJo opened the car door and pulled out the jacket, "See this jacket?"

"Yeah... but I'm still not getting it."

"This was found at the scene of the crime."

"Okay... and?" Moray said, and puffed the cigarette.

"Your business cards were found in the jacket."

"Let me see the jacket," Moray said.

JoJo passed him the jacket. Moray tried putting the jacket on. It was too big. "Okay, this jacket doesn't fit. Now what?"

"Your business cards was found in the jacket," JoJo said then passed him one of the business cards.

Moray looked at the cards. "Yeah, these are the cards. These are the same cards that I made two weeks ago on my computer."

"Whose jacket is this?" Tommy asked.

Moray looked at Tommy with intense eyes. "Now how in the hell would I know some shit like that? I don't know whose jacket this is. Look at it. This is some shit that you young hip-hoppers wear, man. I'm fifty-one years old. Believe me—this ain't my shit."

"So, whose shit is it?"

"I don't know. Somebody has tried to set me up."

"That's for damn sho," Tommy said.

"And you see, Mr. Moray, you can very well get your fuckin head blown off for some shit that you claim you don't know anything about," JoJo said.

Moray threw his hands up. "I don't know anything about this shit. Really, I don't."

"Okay, cool. You don't know anything about this shit, but you know somebody. Who the fuck have you given a card to?" Tommy asked.

Moray put his hand underneath his chin.

Tommy pulled out his 9 mm, but didn't point it.

"What the hell is going on here?"

"Moray, my girl was raped by the same muthafucka that robbed his sister."

"I remember giving some cards to this nigga in the pawn shop ... short, rough- looking guy with braids. Real grimy looking cat. Looked almost like a crackhead."

"This guy was dark skinned?" Tommy said.

"How do you know?" Moray asked.

"I seen him," Tommy said. "The nigga had me tied up."

"Well, if you seen him, you know that I'm not who you're looking for."

"We know that, but we know you might know who he is."

"Let me see the jacket again," Moray asked.

JoJo passed the jacket to Moray.

He hesitated before speaking. "You know what? This is my son's jacket."

"Who is your son?"

"My son Lee ain't no robber, though. The nigga is a square."

"We didn't ask you this; I just want to know who your son is."

"Hey, man, like I said, my son ain't no robber."

"Let us be the judge of that," JoJo said angrily.

Moray pulled his cell phone out then dialed his son's number.

His son answered the phone. "Yeah?"

"Yeah, my ass. I want to know why the fuck was your jacket at the scene of a robbery."

"What jacket?"

"Your *Phat Farm* jacket."

"I haven't seen that jacket in almost two weeks."

"Did you loan it to somebody."

"No, not that I remember."

"Somebody is trying to set you up, Lee," Moray said.

JoJo snatched the phone from him.

"You better explain why the fuck your jacket was at my sister's house or else I'mma fuck your dad up."

126

"I don't know what the fuck you're talking about."

"I'm talking about blowing your daddy's brains out if you don't tell me why your jacket was found at my sister house after it had been broken into."

Moray pulled out another Newport and lit it on the wrong end.

"Hey, let me think."

Tommy cocked the hammer of his gun then put the gun to Moray's head.

"Nigga, did you hear that? My man has the gun up to your daddy's head." JoJo put the phone up to Moray's mouth.

"Son, tell them what you know."

JoJo jerked the phone away from Moray's mouth. "You hear your daddy, don't you?"

"Yeah."

"Okay, what do you know?"

"Jason did it. Jason Black. Do you know him?"

JoJo looked at Tommy and Twin. "Jason Black ... Do this name sound familiar to you?"

"No, not to me," Twin said promptly.

"No, I ain't never heard of him."

"Where the fuck does Jason live?" JoJo asked.

"I don't know, but I can find out," Lee said. "Please don't hurt my old man."

"You got a number I can reach Jason at?"

"Yeah, it's 704-555-8777."

"A'ight. I'm letting your old man go if this number works." JoJo terminated the call then dialed Jason's number. Nobody answered. A Fifty Cent song played on his voice mail. Then JoJo heard a voice. *"Yo, this is Black. Leave your digits and I might hit ya back."*

JoJo dialed again.

This time a man said, "Hello." The same voice that was on the voice mail. "Yeah, this is Black. Who the fuck is this, blowing up my phone?"

"Who the fuck is this?"

"Muthafucka, you called *me*."

"Okay, I need to see you. I think you might know something about a robbery that occurred at my sister's house."

"Nigga, who the fuck is you, and who the hell is yo sister?"

"Can you meet me somewhere?"

"Who are you?"

"I'm Joe, Joe Ingram."

"I ain't meeting nobody unless you got some money. My time is valuable."

"You coward-ass muthafucka."

"Fuck you, nigga. J-Black ain't afraid of nobody. I will fuck you up."

"Bring your guns, nigga."

"I got plenty of them."

Tommy grabbed the phone from JoJo. "Let me speak to him. I know his voice."

"Who the fuck is this?" J-Black said.

"This is the guy you tied up."

"I've tied up so many coward-ass niggas in my day."

"You raped my girlfriend."

"Oh…" Black chuckled. "This is that fat muthafucka from the lake, huh?"

"Exactly. Why don't you meet us somewhere? I need to ask you some questions."

"Fuck you, Nigga. I ain't meeting you nowhere."

"Okay. We got your number; you know we can get your address."

"I don't give a fuck. I ain't running nowhere." He hung up.

Tommy passed the phone back to JoJo.

JoJo called Lee. "I want you to show us where Jason Black lives."

"I can't do that."

"Why?"

"Because he will kill me. That's why."

"Hey, man, this shit ain't worth it," Twin finally said. "I mean, we're making money again; let's leave this alone."

"Either you show us where this nigga live or we gonna hurt your dad, nigga."

Moray looked as if he was about to run.

"Where are you?"

"Carwash on Clanton Road."

"I'll be there in fifteen minutes."

CHAPTER 18

Lee was driving an old black pickup truck. He resembled Moray, except he was taller and wore glasses. He hopped out of the truck.

Twin was the first to approach him. They shook hands. "You think this Black nigga is dangerous, huh?"

"Yeah, man. This muthafucka is a loose cannon, man. He will seriously hurt somebody."

"Twin, why are you acting like a pussy, man?" Tommy asked.

"I ain't acting. I just want to know what we up against."

"I don't give a fuck what we up against; we got a Glock 9, two .45 street sweepers, and shit that will blow your whole back out."

"Man, we're making money. If we kill this muthafucka, we going to jail and ain't nobody going to have shit."

"But if we let him get away, this muthafucka is going to think he can take from us," Tommy said.

"Show us where J-Black lives," JoJo said to Lee.

*****

Black was across the street from his home, inside an abandoned house, watching, looking out the window for any unusual activities. He'd been threatened. He'd been taught from his years in the pen to take every threat seriously. The last time he'd taken a threat lightly, it had cost him a razor wound across the neck while on the inside. He'd been extorting a loan shark named E, taking twenty-five percent of his receivables until D-Rock came on the yard. D-Rock told E not to give J-Black anything, and that he was going to slice his throat if he extorted E again.

E had gone about two months without giving up percentages. When J-Black's commissary got low he finally approached E and took half the commissary in his locker. Later that evening, when J-

Black was on the recreation yard, D-Rock crept up and slashed his neck. Black received eighty-eight stitches. He was also put in solitary confinement because he had refused to name the assailant. The scar was a reminder that he wasn't invincible. He vowed that nobody would ever catch him off guard again.

He lit a cigarette and loaded his sawed-off pump shotgun. He wasn't in the mood to die—not today. This isn't the way his book would end. There would be no one to carry on his legacy. He didn't have kids. His mother had died while he was on the inside.

Only a few cars passed by. Most were going to old man Roscoe's house to get a sack of weed. Black lit another cigarette and was just about to cross the street when a black pickup truck drove down the street. He smiled because he recognized the truck. It was coward-ass Lee. He saw Lee slow down and point at his house.

An SUV full of black men slowed and finally stopped in front of the building. J-Black recognized Tommy and Twin. *Okay, that bitch-ass Lee is showing these niggas where I lay my head.* He wanted to run out there and blast at the truck but decided against it because he was only packing a shotgun, and they probably had automatic weapons.

*****

Exactly nine days later, JoJo received a call from Robert Moray at 6:30 in the morning. He talked to Moray for a few minutes, half asleep.

Moray said, "My son Lee is in the hospital. He was shot by J-Black."

"What?" JoJo said, then stood and walked across the room with the cordless phone.

"Yeah, he's been shot in his ass."

"What ... when did this happen?"

"It happened last night. He was out with his friend at the pool hall down the street from my house. J-Black came up to him after the others left and said he'd seen Lee show y'all where he lived. Words were exchanged and J-Black went back to his car and got a shotgun. Lee ran, but he still managed to get hit."

"Is he okay?"

"Yeah, he's okay, but he's probably going to need physical therapy."

"Well, that's good." JoJo sat back on the bed.

"That's not good. This man shot my son, and he sent word to y'all that he knows where you live, and that he's going to get y'all if it's the last thing he does."

"Fuck him. I don't give a fuck about him."

"Hey, I'm just relaying the message."

*****

Jennifer sat in the kitchen drinking an apple martini. Morgan came over with some Nike pills that had been stolen from the crew. They sipped Martinis and popped pills until they both were horny as hell.

Morgan rubbed Jennifer's thighs and got a rush from it.

Though Jennifer was a stripper, she'd never been with another woman, which was something she prided herself on. She moved Morgan's hand from her leg. "I don't fuck with women."

Morgan looked a little annoyed. "I don't fuck with women, either, but I'm feeling so good, I just want to kiss you. You're so beautiful. I feel beautiful. Can I just rub your thigh?"

Jennifer looked at Morgan for a second. "My boyfriend might come in."

"We'll let him join. Come on. What man wouldn't want to join two blondes?"

"Let's go upstairs and get my toys."

Upstairs, Jennifer got a dildo and stripped to her panties.

Morgan had taken all of her clothes off. She walked over, put her arms around Jennifer, and kissed her neck before Jennifer turned and french kissed her.

They kissed slow and passionately before reaching the bed.

Jennifer lay on the bed with her legs spread apart.

Morgan took the dildo and pushed it in Jennifer's vagina.

"Harder and faster," Jennifer said. "Right there. That's the spot. That's the spot.

Morgan moved the dildo in and out of Jennifer. She was actually feeling pleasure from it, but it wasn't the same kind of pleasure she was used to. She liked for a man to just take control of her and throw her around, pull her hair, slap her ass, and bite her nipples.

Morgan stopped, put her head between Jennifer's legs and performed oral sex.

Jennifer humped Morgan's face three times before saying, "Stop."

"What's wrong?" Morgan asked, confused.

"Nothing's wrong. It's just that I prefer a man."

"Well I prefer you."

Jennifer stood and put her panties back on. "That's your problem. I like men and there is nothing you can do for me, dear."

"You know what? You're a really selfish bitch," Morgan said.

"Whatever."

Morgan stood and put her clothes on. She left without saying a word.

Jennifer was still horny. She called Twin but didn't get an answer. She figured he was out in the street, hustling his drugs.

After a few minutes of fantasizing, she grabbed her cell phone and called Mark.

*****

At three o'clock in the morning, Jennifer lay in Mark's bed. Neither said anything. Both had enjoyed the sexual experience, but there was nothing to talk about. She finally stood and said, "I have to be going. I got a man, you know?"

Mark looked at the clock. "Yeah. I know."

She got dressed then looked in Mark's eyes. "How do you feel about me?"

"I like you. I like you a lot."

"All you can say is *you like me a lot*?"

He stood and put on his boxers "What do you want me to say? You have a man."

"A man that I am betraying for you, so that you can eventually put him away. Then where does that leave me?"

Mark turned his back to her. "I don't understand what you want me to say."

"So, am I just your little sex toy, Agent Pratt? All you want me for is my tits and ass?"

"No, Jennifer ... I like you a lot. I want you to get out of the dancing business and make a new life for yourself."

"Well, I'm going to probably have to get out of the dancing business 'cause once Twin and his boys go down, my ass is going to be wanted."

"Twin ain't no fuckin mobster. These guys are punks."

She sat on the bed and put her stilettos on. Then she stood and walked toward the door.

He jumped up, put his socks on and noticed a pill on the floor. He picked up the pill and, after examining it, he noticed a dolphin on it. "Jennifer, wait." When he entered the living room, she was about to open the front door. "Still using X, huh?"

"What the fuck do you think?"

"I think you shouldn't bring this shit to my house. Don't you know I'm the DEA? You are showing me no respect."

"And you can just fuck me with no feelings ... talking about respect."

"You have a boyfriend."

"Yeah, a boyfriend that I've been lying to and ratting on."

"So where'd you get the X?"

"Mark, can you stop being a policeman and let's talk?"

"About what?"

"Talk about us."

"What about us?"

"Do you love me?"

He didn't say anything; he just looked at the pill.

"Okay, that's what I thought. I've gotta be going."

He ran to the door and blocked it. He wouldn't let her leave. "You know I love you, but I'm not *in love* with you, okay? We've slept together twice. How can you love somebody like that?"

"I don't think you could see yourself with somebody like me ... a little stripper girl, white trash ... Probably afraid of what your friends would think—your dad and that gay-ass partner of yours."

"I don't care what anybody says about me; I'm my own man."

"Don't you see? After Twin is gone, I won't have nobody, nobody to help me."

"Hey, I understand, but I need you to set some goals. And for God's sake, leave these drugs alone." He held up the pill.

She reached for it but he wouldn't give it to her. "Where did you get that from?"

"You must have dropped it. Do you want to tell me where you got it from?"

She looked away. "This is the new drug. They are dealing X now."

"Whoa!" Mark couldn't believe it.

She burst into tears.

Mark held her, kissing her forehead, telling her it was going to be alright.

CHAPTER 19

The next day, Mark had sent her a text message and asked her to meet him at *Dean & Deluca's*, downtown. He'd mentioned that he wanted to take her somewhere. They had a cup of coffee and then hopped into his car.

He took her to the Adam's Mark Hotel and they ended up in one of the conference rooms. A tall, attractive black woman with long, dark hair stood at the front of the room. A huge banner hung in the background. *Dare to Dream: an empowerment seminar for women.*

"What the hell am I here for?" Jennifer asked.

"Just to hear this woman's story; it's incredible."

After everyone was seated, the woman began. "Hello, everybody. My name is Dream Nelson and I have HIV. I just wanted to say that first."

A series of murmurs flowed from the crowd.

Jennifer nudged Mark. "I'm still not understanding." Jennifer couldn't believe the woman had HIV. She looked so beautiful. Her skin was flawless; her teeth were straight; and she was dressed so well.

Dream continued. "First of all, I want to say that I had a very privileged life growing up. Both my parents were educators, and I went to Catholic school all my life. In fact, I was a teacher as well."

Jennifer sighed as if bored.

"But I had an attraction for bad boys, drug dealers in particular. I don't know what it was, but living on the edge kind of gave me a rush; and my parents warned me to stay away from those bad boys. My friend Keisha warned me." Dream pointed to Keisha, who held up a hand.

"My last boyfriend had me trafficking drugs. And I know some of you are probably wondering how a woman so beautiful and intelligent could get caught up in something like that." Dream Nelson paced a little, taking her eyes off the crowd briefly.

"I had low self esteem. I didn't value myself, and when a certain man came along and told me I was the greatest thing since sliced bread, I loved him, and I loved everything he represented. He showered me with gifts and gave me affection; took me on trips, bought me expensive bags and jewelry, and everything. I know there's someone in this audience that knows this type of man. Dream looked at a couple of younger girls on the front row who were wearing flashy jewelry.

"I got stopped in the airport and was strip searched. The police looked in my vagina for drugs. But did I leave him? No."

One lady in the back raised her hand and asked. "How did you get HIV?"

"Good question," Dream Nelson said. "I will get to that in a minute."

Jennifer watched Dream. She didn't appear to be a drug user, so she figured she'd gotten HIV from a man, probably the drug dealer she was talking about.

"I think too many women are out here suffering from esteem issues. Some of us want to gain weight. Others want to loose weight. Some seek plastic surgery. I'm here to tell you that you don't need validation from a man, and to watch the company that you hang with because they can bring you down. The feds came to me about my boyfriend ... you know, the drug-dealer, the one that told me I was the best thing since sliced bread ... asked me to tell them what I knew about him ... told me that they knew I was taking trips with him to California, and that it was just a matter of time before I went down with him unless I told."

A large black woman with a large mole on her jaw raised her hand and said, "I would have told them everything I knew." She high-fived her friend.

"Most people would have told the feds," Dream said. "Not me. I was in love. In love with a dealer, and I couldn't see not being there for my man. He even murdered somebody, and I didn't say anything about him. Had he lived, I could have gone down with him. But he was killed by the police in a shoot-out."

Her eyes were watery now. "Then came the shock that I'd tested positive for HIV."

An attractive woman on the front row came to her side and grabbed the microphone. "Hello, I'm Ms. Nelson's best friend, Keisha Ferguson. We've been best friends since we were ten years old."

The crowd applauded and Keisha continued. "We're here to get women excited about living and being self-sufficient. I'm not saying you don't need a man, but a man should never determine your self-worth."

Dream Nelson held up a paperback book then said, "*Your Self-worth* is the name of the book that my best friend and I co-authored, and it will give you lessons on esteem issues, the value of your body, why it's best to make him wait for sex, and how sometimes we fix ourselves up to be *characters* for men."

Keisha laughed. "What she means by becoming a character is we sometimes overdo it with the colored contacts, fake nails, and long eyelashes just to be sexy for our man. Not saying we shouldn't be sexy, because if you aren't sexy another woman will be. But don't become something you're not just to please a man." She paused. "Again, the title of the book is *Your Self-worth* and it's going for fifteen dollars," Keisha said. "Now Miss Nelson will answer some questions."

A redhead on the front row raised her hand. "Do you think you made a mess of your life?"

Dream Nelson smiled. "I don't think so. I've made some bad decisions, just like everybody else, but ... I like what my life has become. I'm a bestselling author and lecturer, and a business woman; and I'm helping people all over the world. My books have sold over a million copies."

The fat woman on the front row asked, "Do you miss teaching?"

"Yes and no. I miss the kids, but I'm still teaching in a sense; I'm teaching adults."

The fat woman's friend asked, "Do you hate men?"

Ms. Nelson laughed. "Absolutely not. I love men ... I adore men. It's just that I picked the wrong one and it cost me dearly."

Jennifer raised her hand and was recognized. "Ms. Nelson, first of all, I would like to say that you're beautiful. You look like a fashion model or something. My question is this: How did you go from being a drug dealer's girlfriend that was pampered and spoiled to being as successful as you are?"

Dream Nelson blushed and said, "Thanks for the fashion model compliment. To answer your question, going from a drug dealer's girlfriend to being a successful business woman was not easy. First of all, when I found out I had HIV, I tried to kill myself. I didn't want to deal with life; I didn't want to be here. After all, why me? But when I sat and reflected on all the decisions that I'd made in life, I had to ask myself, why not me? Yeah, my boyfriend Jamal is the reason that I got infected with the virus, but I'm a firm believer that we're ninety percent responsible for what happens to us, and I take full responsibility for what happened to me. Having a great support group of friends and family and living a good, spiritual life will help you with anything. Happiness is not money or fame, but perception," Dream Nelson said. "One more question then I will sign books."

A well-groomed black man in a business suit raised his hand.

Ms. Nelson pointed to him and smiled.

"Do you have a man in your life?"

"Ladies and gentlemen, the man that asked the question is my fiancée of two years. He's also a successful businessman. So you see, I'm very happy."

The crowd applauded.

Dream walked to the back of the room and sat at a table. The book signing line formed quickly.

Three hundred and twelve books were sold. She'd signed in Jennifer's book, *Get out of that situation ...You have to live. Love, Dream.*"

*****

Alicia opened the door and Tommy stood before her. She gave him a kiss and invited him in.

When he sat down he looked a little troubled. "What's worng?"

"Well, I haven't been totally honest with you."

"What do you mean?"

"I have to tell you that I have a woman ... and she's living with me."

She frowned. "Tommy, what the hell is going on here?"

He avoided her eyes. "I didn't know what to tell you. All I know is that I want you, and I was willing to do whatever it takes to get you. I'm sorry I lied."

"So what's up with this girl? Do you love her?"

"I only care about her. We don't even have sex."

"So why do you stay in that situation? Why be with someone that you don't love?"

"I don't know. I think we just got comfortable with each other."

"So what are we going to do now?" She walked to him. "I was starting to like you."

"I like you, too. I mean, I want to be with you."

"So go get your stuff and move in with me."

He laughed but didn't answer.

She looked serious and said, "Hey ... I want you to come live with me."

"I can't do that. We barely know each other. How do you know if you can live with me?"

"I don't, but I do know that I don't want you living with her."

Tommy was silent. He knew he had made a mistake telling her about his girlfriend, but he felt better. He was no longer hiding anything.

"Tommy, do you love her?"

"I already told you I'm not in love with her."

"What's her name?"

"Nia."

"Is she pretty?"

"Yeah."

"Does she look better than me?"

"No."

"Why are you with her, Tommy? You said y'all don't have sex."

Tommy turned and faced Alicia. He remembered the first day they'd met, how she'd played hard to get, her comment about not dating drug dealers, and how she was so confident and secure. How did she go from being so secure to being a very insecure woman? It didn't make sense, but it had happened before. He had met women who said they didn't want to be in a relationship and, as time went on, he had gotten to know them and taken them on dates and bought them jewelry. And the next thing he knew they either wanted to get married or didn't want to let him out of their sight. They would call him every other hour and ask stupid questions: Where you been? Why didn't you answer your cell phone?, Who is that female in the background?, Why can't you spend more time with me? All of this because they'd enjoyed his company and money. He doubted very seriously if they wanted him for sex.

"Hey, I'm going to handle the situation."

"How?"

"I'm going to get my own place."

Alicia smiled. "That's what I want to hear."

*****

Tommy had five hundred thousand dollars. He was halfway there. He agreed that Alicia's father would fly into town, get the money, and put it in a safe place. He didn't know why, but he trusted Don with his money. All he kept thinking about was the fact that he would own a high-rise building. He would be an investor in something legal. He could leave the game alone for sure. It was funny how he was thinking about retiring; he was making faster money than ever before with the pills. Everybody wanted X, and he'd become the city's largest X dealer.

He'd taken the money to Alicia's house but was back at home by two in the morning.

Nia had been out with her friends. She didn't arrive until later in the morning.

He heard her tiptoeing into the house. "Where the fuck have you been?" he asked

"I was out with my friend Rasheeda."

"Til five in the morning?"

"It is not five in the morning."

Tommy looked at the clock on the dresser. "Okay, it's 4:30. What the fuck is the difference? The bottom line is that you're being disrespectful."

"*I'm* disrespectful, nigga? You're disrespectful. We get robbed, I get raped for your ass, and all you can think about is the fact that I like to party with my friends?"

"All you think about doing is running the streets."

"You be at the clubs, too."

Tommy walked closer, rubbed his chin, and then pointed at her. "The difference between me and you is that I fuckin own this place. You don't pay shit, so you need to go home."

"Fuck you! I'll go home and never come back to this fuckin place."

"Go home, then."

"You know what? I know that's what you want, so I'm going to stay just 'cause you want me to go."

Tommy went to the bedroom closet and started pulling out Nia's clothes and throwing them all over the floor. "You're going to leave here or I'm going to leave. It's one or the other."

Nia ran over to Tommy and punched him in the face.

"You better leave then, muthafucka."

"I will," Tommy said.

CHAPTER 20

The next morning Nia called JoJo at 10:30 a.m. Agent Pratt and the transcriber listened.

"The nigga left early this morning," said Nia.

"Where'd he go?" asked JoJo.

"I don't know, but I sure as hell hope he stays."

"What happened, baby?"

"I don't know. I came in and he just flipped."

"You think he knew we was together?"

"No, but I know he kind of felt that I was with a man."

"Why?"

"Because I didn't get in until five in the morning. The man is not stupid."

"I know he ain't stupid; that's why I don't like doing this behind his back."

"I know. We need to come out and let everybody know about our feelings for each other. We can't go on like this."

"I can't right now. We're making money together and things are going so well."

"JoJo, I love you, and Tommy just ain't doing it for me. I want you. I mean, every time I have to lay with him it just totally disgusts me. I don't even want him to touch me."

"I promise it won't be like this forever, baby. I have a plan."

"We're going to live together one day?"

"We will. I promise you. If things continue to go good I will be a millionaire in a few more months, and Tommy might be worth at least three."

"I don't care about the money. I don't want to be with him anymore. I want you."

"Well, why didn't you leave?"

She hesitated. "I don't know; I guess I've gotten comfortable with the living situation. That and the fact that I don't want to be alone. I don't know what you're going to do. I don't know if you're just playing with my feelings or what. Tommy is kind of like a security blanket to me, and he's not a bad guy... really he's not. But he's just not for me."

*****

The three Porsche Cayenne trucks were parked in front of a Charlotte night club. Women standing in line marveled at the trucks, wondering who the owners might be. Tommy, JoJo, and Twin were in VIP with six bottles of champagne and a herd of women, celebrating the arrival of more ecstasy. The whole town was going wild over the butterflies. Tommy couldn't supply enough of them.

Alicia came in the club wearing a tight white dress that clung to her every curve. Tommy was aroused immediately. He doubted very seriously that she had on any panties, and this made him even more aroused. Mario, the huge Italian bouncer, allowed her beyond the velvet rope.

She hugged Tommy immediately.

Twin and JoJo stared, their mouths agape.

Tommy introduced Twin and JoJo then said, "These are my best friends in the whole world."

Alicia smiled, revealing beautiful teeth. She shook their hands, and then she and Tommy headed for a private corner.

"Damn, you are looking delicious tonight."

"I know ... you're looking at me like I'm a steak or something." She smiled.

He rubbed her thigh.

She slapped his hand. "Stop it before you get something started that you can't handle."

"Oh, I can handle it. I can handle you."

She toyed with her hair. "Is that so?"

He kissed her neck. His erection occasionally jumped.

She rubbed his chest then hooked a leg behind one of his.

She pulled his penis out and stroked it.

He was enjoying himself until he saw a familiar face in the crowd.

J-Black was looking over the velvet rope with a hard, cold stare.

Tommy pushed Alicia aside, zipped his slacks, then walked over to JoJo and Twin. "That's the guy that robbed me."

"Then that must be the muthafucka who broke into my sister's house and stole my shit," JoJo said. He walked toward the velvet rope.

J-Black raised his shirt, revealing a chrome handgun.

Tommy's heart raced and nervousness set in. He rushed back to Alicia and ordered her to leave the club. Neither he nor his crew was armed. He flagged Mario and informed him that J-Black was carrying a gun. He felt kind of like a snitch for saying something, but he wanted to be smart. He knew that the man who had robbed him was serious, and that it was possible, too, that he would let off a couple of rounds in the club. Somebody could be seriously hurt.

Mario came from behind and held J-Black with a half nelson hold, and one of the other bouncers kicked him then took the gun off him.

J-Black screamed, "Somebody is going to get hurt bad in this bitch. I promise you!"

When they got him to the front door, they tossed J-Black out head first.

He slowly picked himself up and went to his car. He retrieved his sawed-off pump shotgun and opened fire in the direction of the club.

The crowd ran for cover.

Tommy, Twin, and JoJo remained in VIP. None of them wanted to go outside. They knew it was J-Black who had done the shooting.

*****

When Tommy and his partners finally stepped outside the club, J-Black was in handcuffs. A police officer was pushing his head down, ordering him to get inside the squad car.

"I'm glad they got that crazy muthafucka," Tommy said.

"I want the nigga dead," JoJo said.

"The police got his ass. Let's keep making this money," Twin said. He walked to his new Porsche Cayenne truck, got inside and fired it up. "See y'all tomorrow," he said then pulled off.

Tommy leaned against his own new truck. "I want him dead, too, but I got so much shit on my mind right now..."

JoJo caught Tommy's eyes and stared. "What's wrong man?"

Tommy looked away but didn't say anything.

"Come on, Fatboy, you can tell me what's going on with you."

"I think Nia is fuckin around on me."

"You think so?"

"Yeah."

"What about this new chick you been fucking around with?"

Tommy turned and faced JoJo, and then smiled. "I like her a lot."

"So you shouldn't give a fuck about Nia."

"I know, right? But it's hard not to feel a certain way about a woman that I live with. I guess the fact that she's getting over on me and I can't do nothing about it makes me crazy."

"Why don't you just make her leave?"

"She won't leave."

JoJo put his hands on Tommy's shoulders. "You got some serious problems."

"I got a love-hate relationship with Nia."

"I know what ya mean."

"I still love that girl … I mean, we been through a lot, but I still like her in my bed near me. You know what I mean?"

"Yeah… yeah. I know exactly what you mean."

"I don't like to be alone. I mean, I've always had a woman in my life, and I like Nia living with me. Ever since Mama died, she's kind of filled a void."

"I think you should get to know Alicia. Forget about Nia, 'cause she will drive you to do something you might regret."

"I know. When she came in late the other night, it was about five in the morning. I know she'd been with somebody else."

"You think so?"

Tommy's voice was thick with emotion. "I know it, man. You know how sometimes you just get a gut feeling about something?"

JoJo stared off into the dark sky.

"JoJo, I could've killed me a muthafucka that night. I was just that mad."

"Tommy, it's going to be alright."

"I just feel like I'm trapped. I know this girl is no good for me, and I know I like Alicia, but I don't know what to do. It's like Nia has a stronghold on me."

"You can make it, man. Don't let this get you down. Just think … you're about to be a millionaire in no time."

Tommy hugged JoJo. "Thanks for listening to me, man. It meant a lot."

*****

When Twin arrived at his home it was three in the morning. He went to the kitchen for a glass of orange juice and found a note on the refrigerator.

My Dearest Brandon,

I have had some great times with you, and memories that I will probably carry with me for the rest of my life, but great times and memories don't equal love. While I have loved you with my whole heart, I know you couldn't have possibly loved me. If you did, you wouldn't continue to put my life in danger; you wouldn't continue to sell that poison; and you would have spent more time with me and not have taken my love for granted.

In the past year we haven't done anything together. No amusement park, no trips ... except for your business trips. This thing, or relationship, or whatever you call it, had to come to an end, and I have decided it was best that I end it. I've packed all of my belongings. I've got my own place. I believe, when you really think about it, it will be best if we were apart, because we both are sick people. You're sick for pushing the poison, and I'm sick because I'm a recreational user. Don't attempt to call me, because I've changed my number.

Love Jennifer

Twin balled the letter up then slammed his fist against the wall. "I dare that bitch to say I'm pushing poison! I dare that bitch to say I'm sick! I dare the stankin ho to leave! Ain't nobody leaving nobody! I will hunt her ass down and bring her back home. Ain't nobody just going to kick me to the curb like that."

He climbed up in the attic and pulled out a huge green chest. He counted his money and discovered that eighteen thousand dollars was gone. He didn't know where to begin to look for Jennifer. He thought about calling her parents. He hated them. They were a bunch of rednecks.

He didn't want to call Barbara, but he had to. His money was gone and so was Jennifer. Twin dialed Barbara's number.

She answered it on the second ring. "Who the hell is calling me at this time of night?"

Twin figured that old Barb had been hitting the bottle again. "I'm looking for Jennifer."

"Is this the nigger?"

"Fuck you, Barbara. Where the hell is your daughter?"

"If I knew I wouldn't tell you, nigger."

"Have you seen her at all?"

"No, I sure haven't, nigger."

"Tell her to call me if you see her."

"I will not, nigger."

"Fuck you, you trailer trash."

"Nigger, nigger, nigger, nigger!"

Twin ended the call. He would have to find Jennifer some other way.

*****

Jennifer's new apartment was downtown. She'd taken the eighteen thousand dollars, using a portion to furnish her place and pay the rent up for the entire year. She hated stealing Twin's money, but she needed the money for a new start. Her plan was to become a dental assistant, relying on an eight-week course at Central Piedmont Community College. Then she would enroll to become a hygienist. She would dance only when she needed money badly. She would stay away from X and find herself a man who appreciated her, and they would get married and have a big family.

Her biggest challenge, she knew, would be getting off the X. It had her and she craved it. It just made her feel absolutely amazing. It had been sixteen hours since her last pill, and she wanted to go at least a day. She lay in her bed with no entertainment. The cable wouldn't be on until Monday, and the stereo system she had ordered wouldn't arrive until next week.

An hour passed before she decided she needed a pill. It had been seventeen hours and four minutes. She opened her drawer and pulled out the aluminum foil packet. There were six butterflies and one Mercedes. She contemplated then decided she would throw the pills away. The Mercedes pill was the first one to be flushed. This was easy because they weren't the best. She threw five butterflies down the toilet but couldn't bring herself to flush the last one. She swallowed the pill and an hour later she was lying on her bed naked with a vibrator and a glass of vodka and cranberry juice. She worked herself over with the vibrator. Then she called Agent Pratt.

He picked his cell phone up on the second ring. "Hi."

"Hey, sexy! I need some company."

"What do you mean you *need some company*?"

"I left him."

"You're kidding."

"Cut the talking. Just come see me. I live downtown at the Cotton Mill lofts. Come see me. I'm horny."

Mark Pratt held the phone but didn't say anything.

"Pratt ... are you there?"

"Yes. Yes."

"What's wrong?"

"I don't think this is a good idea."

"What? You don't like pussy?"

"Come on. Don't ask me questions like that."

"Just come over. I want you to see my new place."

"I can't."

"What? What the hell are you talking about, you *can't*? First you tell me to leave him, and now you can't come see me? What kind of shit is this?"

Mark Pratt sighed as if he were thinking. Finally he said, "I'm on my way but I can't stay long."

"Hey, I didn't say you had to stay long; I just wanted to see you."

CHAPTER 21

Jennifer greeted Mark at the door, naked. She extended her arms as if she wanted a hug.

He walked around her.

She closed the door then frowned. "What's wrong, officer?"

He didn't respond. Instead, he examined her place. An expensive apartment with very high ceilings. He walked over to the window and looked out into the city. *Excellent view of the skyline*, he thought. Then he examined the furniture. Italian leather. "So, I see you're still living the good life."

"What the hell is that supposed to mean?"

"Nothing. It's just that if you're serious about getting away from that lifestyle, you're going to have to change your thinking."

She walked toward him slow and seductively. "So I guess you want me to live in a shack."

His eyes briefly focused on her breasts then her vagina. He said a silent prayer, asking God for strength. "No, I didn't say that. But I thought you would have tried to budget your money so you can stop dancing."

"I did. I paid my rent up for a year, and I paid for my furniture, and I enrolled in community college ..."

Mark smiled. "Smart girl."

She grabbed his penis print.

"Stop it."

She unzipped his pants.

He tried to pull away from her, but she had already slid his penis out, and seconds later her mouth had covered it.

*****

Twin made his way to the Uptown Carousel and found Morgan.

They walked to the back of the club and sat in a booth.

"What the fuck is going on with your girl?"

"I don't know. What are you talking about?"

"I want to know where the fuck she at, and where the fuck my money's at?"

Morgan looked shocked. "Jennifer ran off with your money?"

"Hell yeah. And the bitch is going to pay when I find out where she at. I ain't playing. I will fuck her up."

Morgan shrugged her shoulders. "I don't know where she's at. I'll tell her when I see her that you're looking for her, but she hasn't been at the club in a day or so."

"I don't know what made her just up and leave like this. Did you have any idea that she was going to leave me?"

"No! She never said anything to me; I mean, never! I think Jennifer will be back."

"Well, I hope so 'cause she took eighteen grand from me, and that's enough for me to hurt a muthafucka. You know what I mean?"

"Hell yeah."

"Hey, listen. If you can find her and let me know where she's at, I'll give you a little reward."

Morgan smiled. "What did you have in mind?"

"A hundred dollars."

"I don't need money. I need some pills. Give me ten butterflies and I'll find her for you; I promise."

Twin looked at Morgan, disgusted. She was nothing but an X head, just like Jennifer. Someone he should have never involved himself with. "Okay, Morgan. If you find her I'll give you some pills."

*****

"What the hell is that on your neck?" Ken asked.

"What are you talking about?" Mark pretended to study papers on his desk.

"There's a mark on your neck. You must have slept with a vampire last night or... let me guess ... the stripper-slash-informant that I warned you about."

Mark pulled his collar up, trying to cover the mark. He couldn't believe he had let the woman bite his neck. He couldn't believe he had been exposed. He wanted to lie to Ken.

"The stripper got to you, huh?"

Mark made eye contact with Ken. "Shut up, man; will ya?"

"Hey don't get on my case. You need to talk to your little vampire woman. She's the one that bit your neck."

Mark rose from his desk. "I think I'm going to get out of here before I hurt you."

"Hurt me? I'm just trying to help you, man. I don't want you to be involved with a chick like that. You don't need her, man."

"I don't need your help. I don't need anything from you."

"This chick is going to bring you down. She's going to cause you to lose your job."

Mark opened the door and stepped out into the hallway.

Ken followed. "So do you love her, Mark?"

"What are you talking about?

"Do you love Jennifer?"

Mark turned and faced him. "I don't know," he said, almost inaudibly.

*****

Jennifer opened the door wearing a sequined dress that clung to her geometry. She met Mark with a kiss and immediately unbuttoned his shirt. He pulled away from her.

"What's wrong?" she asked.

"I don't know. I think I'm falling for you."

"And you're saying that like it's a bad thing."

He sat down on her sofa. "I told you from the start that I didn't think it was a good idea that we be sleeping around together."

She walked across the room. "You're the one that came to the club. You're the one that sought me out, Mr. DEA. What was I? Some kind of sick fantasy of yours, and now that you've fucked me the fantasy no longer arouses you? Huh?"

"No."

"What is it then? Why can't I have you? Why can't we be together?"

Mark sighed. "I don't know. I just don't think it's a good idea."

"What happened to all of this shit you were saying ... that you were going to help me, and that I needed to get away from the lifestyle? What happened to that shit?"

He stood and faced her. He looked at her breasts. Her waist was so damn tiny. He thought about the sex they'd had last night, and an erection was on the way.

"So, I guess now that I left Twin, I'm on my own."

Mark looked away. He didn't want to be tempted by her. He had to get his mind focused. "Yes. You have to take care of yourself."

"I don't understand this shit, man. Last night you come over and we make passionate love, and now you leave me."

"I'm not leaving you. I'm going to be there for you. But not... sexually."

"I'm not good enough for you, huh?"

"No. I didn't say that."

"You don't have to say that. I know what you mean." Tears rolled down her cheeks.

Before he realized it, he was holding her.

She looked up at him then jerked away.

"Jennifer, it's not like that."

"You know what, Agent Pratt? I'm a big girl. I can take care of myself. How about you just get the hell out of my house, please."

Mark walked to the door and let himself out.

*****

Tommy found him a nice apartment but spent most of his nights with Alicia. He had convinced himself that he wasn't going back to Nia and that they weren't meant for each other. He had started out spending the night, bringing a change of clothes. Now all of his things were in her extra closet. He would move all his things into his place by the end of the month because he could feel her getting attached, and he needed his space. He had just got out of the shower and was putting on his clothes, about to go deliver some butterflies on the west side of town.

She stopped him and asked, "Are we going to spend the day together?"

"I got to handle some business, baby," he said then kissed her on her cheek.

"Tommy, you're always in the streets."

"What are you talking about? I was with you yesterday, re-member? We went to the park together and went to dinner."

"But that's not enough, one dinner; I want to be with you more."

Tommy sighed. Alicia was starting to sound a lot like Nia, with all the bitching and complaining, but actually he hadn't been around lately because the pills had become big business for him. Never was he required to work so hard in the streets—not even for coke. "I tell you what. Let's take a trip to San Fran to see your dad," Tommy said.

She smiled then gave him a hug

*****

At JoJo's apartment, Twin, JoJo, and Tommy planned another trip to Miami.

"I still haven't found that bitch with my eighteen G's. It's been two weeks."

"You may as well get over it. You ain't going to get your money back," JoJo said.

"I wouldn't want it back. You should just be glad the bitch is out of your life," Tommy said.

"Yeah, I think your girl is bad news."

"Why do you say that?" Twin quizzed.

"She took your money, nigga. What else do you we need to say?"

"She wasn't all bad," Twin said.

"What was good about her?" Tommy asked.

"The fact that her and her friend was willing to bring our shit back from Miami."

"Yeah, that's true," Tommy said.

"So who's going to bring it back now that we don't have her?" JoJo asked.

Tommy thought long and hard. He would have volunteered, but he knew he was down to the last two trips. He would be a millionaire. He would have the money needed to invest in real estate, and he just couldn't chance it. "I don't know," Tommy finally said.

"Okay ... you can still use Jennifer's friend."

"Yeah. She still needs money. You know how those strippers go through money," Twin said. He picked his cell phone up and dialed her number.

"Hello," Morgan said.

"Hello," Twin said. "Hey—just wanted to know if you wanted to go to Miami with us."

"To make some money, I hope."

"Yeah. Of course. That's what I called you for."

"Cool, because I just bought a new motorcycle, and the insurance is kicking my ass."

"So have you heard from my girl?"

Morgan didn't say anything.

"So have you seen Jennifer?"

"Yeah, Twin, I've seen her."

"Why didn't you tell me? I thought we had an agreement?"

"Yeah, we did, but she made me promise not to tell you. I think she's ready to come back home."

"Is she really?"

"Things just ain't working out for her. I mean, she has this fabulous apartment downtown, but she just ain't happy,"

"So who's the new man?"

"There ain't no new man."

"Why did she leave?"

"I don't know, Twin. I guess you wasn't giving her the attention she needed."

"I gave that bitch everything—diamonds, minks, new cars and shit; and the bitch still wasn't happy."

"Money don't make everybody happy."

"It sure as hell makes me happy."

"So when are we leaving for Miami?"

"In the morning."

"Cool. I'll get packed."

"Morgan, you still haven't told me where Jennifer's living."

"She lives downtown at the Cotton Mill lofts, number 2131. Please don't tell her that I told you where she's living."

"Thank you, Morgan. Goodbye." Twin terminated the call.

"So is Morgan going to help us?" Tommy asked.

"Yeah, but I got better news than that," Twin said.

"Tell us what's going on?" JoJo said.

"Morgan just told me where Jennifer is."

"What the fuck are you waiting on then. You need to go to her house and demand your money," Tommy said.

"I know. I'd already be at her fucking door," JoJo said.

Twin stood. "I'm on my way over there now."

"Okay, don't go over there and get your ass locked up." JoJo said.

"Listen. We got to be smart, man. You can't go over there and fuck her up over eighteen thousand dollars and bring the heat on us," Tommy said.

"Fuck. The heat is already on us," Twin said. "You remember, this is the bitch that told us the heat was on us."

"But she knows too much is all I'm saying."

"I feel you," Twin said.

CHAPTER 22

Jennifer screamed when she stepped out into the hallway.

Twin grabbed her wrist. He pushed her back into her loft then covered her mouth. "Shut the fuck up, bitch. I hope you didn't think you would get away with my money, did you?"

"What are you talking about?"

Twin looked around. The loft had very nice hardwood floors. New furniture, a plasma television set, and expensive sculptures. "Where the fuck all this shit come from?"

"I paid for everything in here," Jennifer said.

"Better not have been with my money."

"I have my own money."

"Well why in the fuck did you take mine?"

She tried to jerk away from him, but he slung her to the floor.

"Where is my money, Jennifer?"

"You owe me that money."

Twin kicked her in the ribs. "I don't owe you a goddamn thing."

Jennifer held her side then tears came down her face.

Twin kicked her again. "White trash. I will kill your ass, you understand me? When I met your ass you didn't have shit. I gave you the world."

Jennifer stood and faced him. "Muthafucka, you didn't love me. You ever thought about that?"

"How can you say that, Jennifer?"

"All I was to you was your little white show piece. You didn't give a damn about me because if you did, I wouldn't be dancing in the club. A real man wouldn't let his woman dance in the club. And don't say you don't have the money. I've helped you count hundreds of thousands of dollars, often wondering when you would take me out of the clubs."

"I thought you liked earning your own money."

"I do like that, but I don't like men lusting for me night after night, asking me if I will fuck them for five hundred dollars, or will I suck their stinking dicks for a thousand dollars. It's disgusting and demeaning."

"That's the life you chose to lead."

"But you supposed to be my man. How can you let me live like that? And you making all that damn money... " she said, her mascara leaving a black streak on her face.

"You never said nothing to me about not liking the club."

"Do you like dealing drugs?"

Twin thought for a moment. Though he didn't have any complaints about the benefits, he would rather not do it. Only a fool would want to deal drugs. He didn't answer her.

"So, I take it you don't like dealing," Jennifer said. She sat on the arm of her chair.

Twin turned his back to her. "But this still don't excuse you for taking my shit, Jennifer. You had no fuckin right."

"You're right, Twin, but your money is gone. I don't have it anymore, and there's nothing I can do to bring your money back."

"That's fucked up!"

She walked up to him and put her arms around his waist. "Twin, you know I love you. I've loved you since the first day I saw you, but I don't know what got into me. I guess I got sick of it all."

He turned then stared her in her eyes.

"I miss you."

He pulled away from her. "I don't know if I can forgive you for this one, Jennifer. I mean, I trusted your ass."

"Okay, I took eighteen thousand dollars, but I been with your ass for four years. I've counted thousands of dollars and took thousands of dollars to my mother's house for you, and I've never stole a red cent."

"And that's what's fucked up about the whole situation. I thought you were loyal."

Jennifer threw her arms up in disgust. "Well I can't bring the money back, Twin. What do you want me to do?"

He stared her in her eyes. "I need you to make a run for me. I need you to go to Miami with me to get more X—you and Morgan."

Jennifer sighed. "I don't want to go to Miami; I really don't. But if it's going to make everything okay, I'll go on this one last trip."

"Cool."

"When are we going?"

"Soon."

*****

Tommy and Alicia stepped off the plane in San Francisco.

Don and his driver were there to meet them. This time, instead of the Maybach, it was a stretch Hummer, and it whisked them away to a downtown high-rise apartment—Avalon Towers.

"Daddy, why are we here?" Alicia asked.

"I just bought a penthouse. I want you and Tommy to stay here for tonight."

*****

After gawking at all the penthouse luxuries and amenities, Tommy walked toward the window again. She cut him off. She stood in front of him, grinning. Then she peeled her blouse off. Her nipples were nearly pink, and they were standing at attention.

He leaned into her and they kissed.

"I want to be with you forever, Tommy."

"How can you say that? You barely know me."

She unzipped her jeans. They fell to the floor. She stood before him wearing only the G-string that he'd been straining to see when she turned sideways. "Tommy, make love to me."

His penis was limp. It had never been limp when she tried arousing him. She was the one person who could give him a hard-on instantly.

She kissed him again. Her tongue entered his mouth, searching for his tongue. She pulled out and slobbered on her lip. She laughed. "Tommy, you've got to learn to kiss."

He wiped his mouth. "I'm sorry."

"It's okay, Tommy," she said then she grabbed his crotch.

"What's wrong, baby?"

He stood there for a moment. His mind flashed back to Nia and all the times he couldn't get an erection. All the strippers that he'd paid to have sex with and couldn't perform. He thought about Lisa from Toronto. Every single incident that he couldn't perform came into his mind in a brief moment.

"Tommy, you're not hard." She frowned.

"I know. I'm just not in the mood."

"But *I* am." She kissed him then she grabbed his crotch again. It was unresponsive to her.

She grabbed his hand and led him to the bedroom. In it was a huge sleigh bed with a silk comforter set.

Tommy looked at her ass, but his penis still did not cooperate.

She pulled his pants down. "Tommy, I don't get it. Am I not attractive to you?"

"Hell yeah. You're fine as hell."

She kissed him again, unbuttoned his shirt, and kissed his belly. She made him feel good. He'd always been self-conscious about his weight but he didn't feel fat around her at all.

Her tongue traced his bellybutton.

His penis was still lifeless. He looked down at her beautiful face. He wondered whether her tongue would travel further below the belly button. He didn't think it would, but he couldn't help but wonder how nice it would be to have somebody as beautiful as her perform oral sex on him.

She held him and licked his shaft. Still there was no life in his penis. She put the tip of it in her mouth, but it still didn't get hard. "Tommy, what the fuck is wrong?"

He stood and put his pants on without his underwear.

"Not delicious enough for you anymore?"

Tommy never understood why women always felt the need to be told they were sexy, or why they always took it personal when a man couldn't get his dick hard for them. "No, it's not that at all."

"What is it then, Tommy?"

"Just not in the mood."

"I don't believe that. Something is on your mind."

"Nothing is on my mind."

She put her arms around him.

His heart rate increased. He found himself saying. "I have a problem with erections sometimes."

"Really?" she asked.

"Yeah."

"Why didn't you say something?" She laughed.

"Why are you laughing at me?"

"Not laughing at you, baby. I just find it funny that you were afraid to be honest with me, Tommy. I care about you, not about whether you are able to bump and grind."

He smiled but still avoided her eyes. It was still embarrassing to him that he couldn't get it up.

She told him to lie on his stomach. He complied and she gave him a back massage.

"You are the fuckin coolest," Tommy said.

"Why do you say that, babe?"

"I told you my problem and you're still digging me."

"I think I love you."

"You think?"

"I love you, Tommy." She smiled and continued massaging his back.

He turned on his back. They kissed long and passionately. He gripped her ass and held it.

She put her tongue in his ear.

His penis grew.

She grabbed it and smiled.

His heart rate increased again.

She gave him a small peck on his jaw and said, "Calm down, Tommy. It's going to be okay."

"You think so?"

"I know so," she said. Then she straddled him and sat on his erection.

*****

Don arrived at the penthouse at 8:30 a.m. They all hopped in the Maybach and drove to the International House of Pancakes on Mission Street.

The hostess greeted Don with a warm smile. "Don, it will be a few minutes before we can clear your table."

"Daddy, don't tell me you still sitting at the same table," Alicia said.

"That's where the business goes down." He turned and smiled at Tommy. "We are here to discuss business, aren't we?"

"That's right. I want to own buildings one day."

"I can make that happen for you."

The hostess led them to Don's table. Once they were seated, the waitress appeared and took their order. Tommy ordered pork chops and eggs. Alicia asked for cereal and toast. Don only wanted a cup of coffee.

"Not eating breakfast?"

"Naw, not this morning. I tend to go light on the breakfast or have nothing at all. I suggest you start going light. I mean, you're not going to be young all your life. That pork is bad for you, and those eggs have too much cholesterol. That shit can cause all kinds of problems—heart attacks, strokes, impotence..."

Alicia nudged Tommy under the table.

"Yeah, you're right."

"But back to business. Do you have any more money; we're getting close to the deadline?"

"Yeah. I got another $250,000."

"That's $750,000; we're almost there."

"Yeah. Can't I just go with that? I mean, this is a lot of money."

"Yeah, it's a lot of cash when you're talking in street terms, but now we're talking corporate terms, Tommy. We are going to make millions of dollars. Look at what your return will be on this investment. I mean, I could let you in for $750,000 and your return won't be as high. I want you to get out of this drug game. I want you to be able to take care of my daughter."

"Daddy, I can take care of myself."

"I know you can, baby." Don grabbed her hand and stroked it.

"I should have the money in two weeks."

"You will make $250,000 in two weeks? Perhaps I should invest in *you*," Don teased.

"Yeah. If everything goes right, I will have the money in two weeks."

"Damn. You selling that much coke?"

"No, I don't mess with the coke any more. It's all about the X now. Everybody wants the pills."

"I guess so, if you're telling me that you should have $250,000 in two weeks."

"That will give me the million dollars I need to invest."

"Yeah, it will."

"Then I'm out of the game."

The waitress appeared with the food. Everybody remained quiet until she left.

Tommy sipped his orange juice and said, "Yeah, I'm finished. I've been selling drugs since I was sixteen, and I'm thirty now."

"Never caught a case, huh?"

"I've been blessed to have never caught a case, and I've never had a million dollars at one time because I've always spent my money as I made it. Luckily, you came along with this opportunity. I would have probably still been spending it as I go," Tommy said.

"I still say you don't need the Maybach Benz," Alicia said.

"I need it. You only live once. Right, Don?"

"That's right. Besides, when you're ready, we can lease you one in my company's name."

Alicia put her arms around Tommy's waist. "I just don't want anything to happen to him."

"Nothing is going to happen to Tommy. He's smart. He is investing his money wisely, and he's getting out of the game."

Tommy smiled. He liked the sound of that. He was happy that he was getting out of the game. He was happy he had found some good people who cared about his well-being.

"So, did you bring the money with you?"

"No, I'll send it to you when I get back to North Carolina or, if you prefer, I can wait until I get the other $250,000 and send it all at one time."

"I need what you got now, so that we can clean it up."

"Okay. Makes sense to me."

"Tommy, I'm about to make you a multimillionaire, a legitimate multimillionaire."

"So I can take care of your daughter."

Alicia punched Tommy in his chest. "Stop saying that."

CHAPTER 23

Don had called Tommy and told him to go to the Benz dealership on Independence Boulevard in Charlotte. The car had been leased to RJ Holding Corp, one of Don's corporations.

Tommy sat behind the wheel of the $360,000 car. An older white man driving a 600 Benz looked on with envy. A small crowd gathered outside the dealership, all wondering what black celebrity owned such an expensive car.

"He plays for the Panthers," a thin white woman said. "Yeah, I think he's number 88. I seen him on TV."

"I think he's a rapper," another man said.

Tommy sat behind the wheel in awe of the machinery. He felt like he owned the city.

An older black salesman opened the door and sat on the other side of the vehicle. "Hey, brother, is this car for you?"

Tommy was proud. "Yes. Yes sir, it is."

The man extended his hand. "Man I'm always glad to see one of us on top." He pointed to the back of his hand. "You know ... Blacks."

"Yeah."

"Everyone out there is curious to know what you do for a living."

Tommy frowned. "Why?"

"I guess because of the car, man. This ain't no ordinary car."

"I know, but my company's leasing it."

"Bro, this car is worth over three-hundred thousand dollars."

Tommy began to wonder if he had made the right decision. He wasn't even off the lot yet and people were talking. They were curious. He wondered how long it would take before the feds found out that Tommy Dupree was riding around in a mobile mansion. He wouldn't concern himself with that. He couldn't worry about it. Tonight he would have some fun.

Tommy put his hands on the steering wheel. He felt like a sixteen year old kid who had just obtained his license. He just wanted to ride—anywhere.

"Bro, I hope I'm not being too nosey, but how are you getting your bread?"

"I'm a real estate investor," Tommy said, feeling confident.

*****

Tommy pulled up at JoJo's apartment, called him from his cell phone, and told him to come outside.

Minutes later, JoJo stood before Tommy. "Nigga, are you out of your fucking mind?"

"What are you talking about?"

"This car is what I'm talking about. I told you not to get this damn car."

"It's totally legit. I mean, everything is in Alicia's dad's name."

JoJo shook his head in disbelief. "Tommy, I can't believe you are so stupid, man. You've always been a little smarter than the average. If you had been Twin, I would have totally understood … but I can't believe you, man."

"You only live once. Get in here, man. You ain't gonna believe this car."

JoJo sat in the passenger seat. "These seats are plush and comfortable."

"Can you believe the room in this muthafucka?"

JoJo looked around. "Damn, you got a laptop hooked up in the backseat."

"I know, man. The first time I got into one of these muthafuckas I knew I had to have one."

"I thought you said Alicia's dad leased you the car."

"He did."

"Well it ain't yours then, technically; it's his."

"Yeah, but we're partners."

JoJo didn't respond. He was deep in thought. Tommy wheeled the Maybach out of JoJo's parking lot and hit the freeway about a mile away. He accelerated the car up to almost 100 mph.

"What the fuck are you doing man?" JoJo asked.

"Watch this."

"Watch what, nigga? I ain't trying to die with you."

Tommy pointed to his foot. "Watch how I barely touch the brake."

He placed his foot on the brake lightly and the car slowed to 35 mph in seconds. "I'm telling you, man ... this car is the shit."

"Tommy are you sure about Alicia's dad, man? Do you think you can trust him with your money? I know you sent him some money before, and I know you trying to get out of the game and all, but how can you trust somebody with that much money?"

"The man has money. He don't need shit from me. I need him."

"Okay; whatever you say."

Tommy looked at JoJo, who seemed to be concerned about him. "Listen, man. I know you're worried, but trust me. Everything is going to be okay. We're going to the top. I'm gonna take you to the top with me."

"Say no more."

*****

The Maybach was in front of the Liquid Lounge. Tommy had paid Bernard, an elderly guy from the neighborhood, to drive the car for tonight. Tommy and Alicia sat in the back of the car. Twin and JoJo were in Twin's truck, parked directly in front of the Benz.

Nia and her girlfriend Rasheeda were leaving the parking lot across the street when they spotted the Benz. Nia ran across the street and pressed her face against the back window, determined to see who was inside. "Fat-ass nigga. I know you in there with your bitch."

"Who is that?" Alicia asked.

"That's my ex. The one I used to live with."

"Nigga, you ain't going to fuckin play me like that. I will hurt your ass. I will kill you, nigga," Nia shouted. Nia started pounding on the hood of the car. "Get out of the car, Tommy; I know your ass is in there."

Tommy opened the door, stepped out of the car, and faced off with Nia.

"Nigga, how you gonna play me like this?"

"What the hell you mean? We ain't together no more."

"I know we ain't together no more, but you owe me, muthafucka. I've been with you from day one and this is the fucking thanks I get."

"Fuck you, Nia. You never loved me."

"Fuck *you*, muthafucka," Nia said. She charged at Tommy

swinging wildly.

Twin and JoJo jumped out of the truck. Alicia got out of the car to see what was going on.

Tommy grabbed Nia's arms. "Rasheeda, get your friend before I hurt her."

"Nigga, you've already hurt me. You hurt me with that bitch of yours."

"What are you talking about?"

"You know what the fuck I'm talking about," Nia said with tears rolling down her face.

Tommy shoved Nia. She fell to the pavement. A small crowd gathered.

Nia got up and ran with her head down, clawing at Tommy.

He quickly contained her again. "Nia what the fuck is wrong with you?"

"I was with you from day one. You think I'm going to let somebody take my position?"

"What position?"

"I'm your wife, remember? I've been through a lot with your ass. I'm the one that got raped, not this uppity-ass bitch that don't want nothing but money." Nia pointed at Alicia.

"You don't know nothing about me," Alicia said.

"I know you got my man."

Tommy took a step back, pointed toward the car, and asked Alicia to get inside.

"That's right, bitch. Get inside the car before I fuck you up."

"Nobody is going to do anything to me," Alicia said.

Rasheeda stepped forward. "Don't get yourself hurt out here."

Tommy stared at Rasheeda. She was a big girl with broad shoulders and muscular arms. He knew that Alicia and Nia would have been a good match, but Rasheeda was built like a man. He would have to take her on. He opened the door for Alicia.

She stepped inside the car.

"Tommy, why do you want to destroy everything we had?"

They looked directly at one another. "Nia, you made my life miserable. We never had anything ... nothing ... no kind of chemistry; you know?"

"So it's like that, Tommy? You going to kick me to the curb just like that?" She wiped her eyes.

"Nia, it's over."

Nia dropped her head and charged Tommy again, scratching his face before he knocked her down again.

The crowd roared with laughter and someone yelled, "That bitch is making a fool out of herself."

"Nia, stop. You are making yourself look ridiculous."

Rasheeda walked to her side and held her arm.

"I'm making a fool out of myself? Well now it's time to make a fool out of you."

"Go home, Nia," Tommy pleaded.

"Not before I let you know I been playing your fat ass all along. I even fucked your boy, JoJo. We've been having sex on the regular, and the nigga is good."

Tommy looked at JoJo, who turned his head.

"Is that true, Joe?"

"I don't know what she's talking about."

"Talking about me and you meeting downtown at the Holiday Inn on the regular ... talking about you telling me that you want to be with me, nigga."

"Is that true, Joe?"

"Tell him, Joe. Tell him how we have sex all day and all night. Tell about the time you fucked me in the house when Tommy was out of town."

JoJo looked at Tommy, but he couldn't say anything.

Alicia hopped out of the car, and walked up to Tommy. She held him tightly.

Tommy avoided looking at JoJo.

*****

Tommy stared at J.C. from across the table. J.C. looked as if he'd aged a decade since the last visit. He'd gotten some glasses, and his hair was significantly grayer than before.

J.C. cracked his knuckles. "So, JoJo has been fucking your woman, huh?"

"Yeah," Tommy said then put his elbows on the table and looked around the crowded visiting room. "I can't believe this shit."

"Well, believe it, son. Let me tell you what I've been telling you all along. You ain't got no friends."

"Me, Joe, and Twin grew up together. That's why it hurts."

"I know. But let me tell you something. I told you I ain't never liked that Twin ever since y'all were kids. His brother is a different story. I always knew he would be a good kid. You knew he would amount to something."

"What about Joe?"

J.C. cleaned his glasses with his shirt. "I never thought Joe would do you like that, son."

Tommy sighed. "I know."

"But, Son, when you in them streets, nobody is your friend. You know the old saying: Ain't no honor among thieves."

"I'm starting to figure that out."

J.C. smiled. "Now tell me about this new girl that has been keeping you busy."

"Her name is Alicia. She's from California. Her dad is this big real estate tycoon. He owns a mansion … all types of shit. The man has it going on. In fact, he's showing me how to invest my money wisely …you know, putting it in some real estate."

The smile disappeared from J.C.'s face. "Speaking of being wise, I heard you just got a new car."

Tommy looked surprised. "How did you know that?"

"Man we hear everything in here, I heard you be parking your car in front of the club and shit."

"Yeah, I did once."

"Word in here is that you got the X game on lock."

Tommy didn't say anything. He just stared at his father. He couldn't believe that everything he'd done had been broadcast all throughout the prison system. He thought he was being discreet, but everybody knew his business.

"So, is it true, boy?"

Tommy didn't say anything.

"Nigga, what the fuck is wrong with you? I'm trying to get out of this place and you trying to come in here. I tell you what, I won't be in here when you get here; that's for damn sure."

"What do you mean?"

"Man, as soon as they get those DNA results and check it against the hair fibers found at the scene of the rape, I'm out of here. My trial lawyer never fought for that."

Tommy was happy for him. It had been eight years since his dad had seen the outside world. He had been convicted of raping a white university student. On the night the alleged rape had taken place, the young woman had been jogging, and a tall black man had jumped from behind some bushes and forced her behind a building. J.C. was working at the university at the time. He was waiting on the bus to take him home when the police grabbed him. He hadn't been a free man since. He didn't have the money for adequate representation at trial, so he was convicted and sentenced to twenty-five years.

"I'm telling you, Tommy, I'm close to being a free man again."

"I know, Dad," Tommy said looking away.

"Tommy, look at me."

He looked into the man's eyes.

"Hey, man, the shit you are doing out there ain't you, man. This ain't the life you want to lead. Everybody ain't built for this."

"I know," Tommy said.

"Remember when you were a kid? When me and your mama used to take you fishing? You would jump on my back when we would leave the lake. I think you were about six or seven years old then."

A huge smile appeared on Tommy's face. "Those were the good old days."

"Tommy, I never really had a biological son, only a daughter that I haven't seen since her birth. But you are the only son I knew, the only son that I will ever love. I consider you my blood."

"I know. I feel the same about you, J.C."

"Tommy, don't you want to experience things like carrying your son on your back, and teaching him how to fish?"

"Yeah, of course I do."

"Well then, damn it, act like it!" His eyes were watery and he was oblivious to the onlookers.

Tommy had never seen him so angry.

Two corrections officers came over to the table. The taller one asked, "Is there anything wrong?"

"Naw, just having a discussion with my son."

The guards walked away slowly.

J.C. zeroed in on Tommy again. "I just want you to be at home when I get out. You understand me?"

"Yes, sir ... I understand." A tear rolled down Tommy's face.

J.C. stood, walked over, and hugged him.

Tommy looked up at his father and said, "One more trip."
"Make this your last one, son. Promise me."
"I promise."

CHAPTER 24

When Tommy entered Twin's house and saw JoJo sitting on the sofa, he turned to leave.

"Wait a minute, Tommy. I need to talk to you," JoJo said.

"Fuck you, man. I ain't got shit to say to you, man."

"You are overreacting about this whole situation."

Tommy turned to face JoJo. "I'm overreacting? You supposed to be my man, and I find out that you been fuckin my girl. How am I supposed to feel?"

"Hey, man, I'm sorry about what happened, and I can't change that."

Tommy looked at Twin. "Get this nigga out my face before I punch his goddamn lights out."

"I want y'all to talk this shit over. We are friends, man. Been friends since the sandbox."

"And friends are the very muthafuckas you got to keep your eye on."

"That ain't true, nigga. I won't ever do anything to hurt you. I would never snitch on you. That says a lot in this business," JoJo said.

"Do you like Nia, nigga?"

JoJo turned away.

"You don't have to answer ... you can have the bitch."

"Tommy, don't take this shit too seriously," Twin said.

"When that white bitch took your money, you didn't want nobody to tell you shit," Tommy said.

"What do I have to do with what's going on between y'all?"

"Nothing. That's why I want you to stay the fuck out of it."

"Come on, Tommy; this ain't the end of the world," JoJo said.

Tommy stepped closer and grabbed JoJo's shirt, yanking him up. "Hey, muthafucka, you don't have any idea how I feel. I had this woman in my house, sleeping in the same bed with her night after night, and she's fuckin my best friend—a nigga I would have taken a bullet for."

"Hey, man, let go of my shirt."

Tommy shoved JoJo to the floor.

JoJo sprang up, grabbed a picture frame from the table, and charged at Tommy.

Twin got between them.

"Muthafucka, if you ever put your hands on me again, we're going to be burying your fat ass."

"That will be the day."

"Come on, man, we got one more trip, then we can call it quits. You niggas got to be friends. We need to do business together."

Tommy was fuming and breathing heavily.

JoJo put the picture frame back on the table. "I don't need to be your friend." "Good, because, nigga, we'll never be friends," Tommy said.

"That's fine with me," JoJo said.

*****

At about 2 a.m., Twin heard a loud thud that appeared to come from downstairs. He'd been dozing off in bed. He didn't see Jennifer. Then he remembered that she had gone downstairs to watch television. He called out her name.

She screamed. "Oh God. Help me!"

"Shut up, bitch. I will kill you."

Twin realized he had an intruder in the house. He looked under his mattress for the Taurus 9mm but remembered that he'd left it in his truck. "Fuck!" Why didn't he set the home alarm? He grabbed the phone from the dresser.

"Muthafucka, drop that phone, with your bitch ass."

He recognized the voice. It was J-Black, and he was holding Jennifer by the throat.

"I need money and I need it fast."

"I've given you money already, and I've put you up on licks. And this is the thanks I get?"

"Twin, I don't want to hear that shit. I will kill this white bitch, then I will blast your punk ass if you don't give me no money."

"How did you know where I live?"

176

"Nigga, I'm the best at tailing muthafuckas. Don't you know?"

"Twin give him the money," Jennifer pleaded.

J-Black smiled. "I see why you didn't want me coming here. I guess you didn't want me to see your lily white trophy, huh?"

Twin carefully stepped to his closet and eased out with a shoe box. He dumped the money on the bed. "Five grand is all I have."

"I need more than this."

"I don't have it right now."

J-Black put the butt of his gun in Jennifer's mouth. He moved it in and out. "I bet you suck good dick, don't you?"

She began to gag.

"How about if I make your girl give me some head?"

Twin stared at him and said, "I ain't giving you shit. I'm tired of you extorting me. I ain't got nothing else for you."

J-Black took the barrel out of Jennifer's mouth and aimed it near Twin's head. He pulled the trigger and blew a huge hole in the wall about the size of a small cantaloupe.

Twin hit the floor as if he'd been shot.

The smoke detector went off.

"I'm sure the neighbors heard that," Jennifer said.

J-Black released Jennifer and scooped up the money. "Muthafucka. I will be back. You better have something better for me or else I'm going to tell your boys you're the one that's been having them robbed." J-Black rushed downstairs and hurried toward the back door.

"What is he talking about? You set your friends up?"

"I don't know what the hell he's talking about."

"Twin, did you have Tommy and JoJo robbed?"

Twin sat on the bed and refused to look at her.

"You had your friends robbed?" Jennifer asked again.

"Not quite."

"What do you mean, *not quite*?"

Twin looked Jennifer in the eyes. "J-Black is a crazy muthafucka."

"Tell me something I don't know."

"Well, he threatened to kill me if I didn't give him somebody to rob."

"And now look, he's still threatening to kill you."

"I know."

"Baby, we've got to move or else he's going to come back. I don't feel safe here. Isn't he the one that raped Nia?"

"Yeah."

"And you held all of that in? You didn't tell Tommy that you knew who raped his girl?"

Tears rolled down Twin's face. "Shut the fuck up."

"Are you really his friend?"

"Hell yeah. How can you ask me something like this?"

"Because all you care about is yourself."

Twin put his head between his legs. "Don't everybody think about themselves?"

She didn't answer.

"But, you're right, we have to go. We have to leave here. Let's go to the condo downtown."

*****

They were at an exclusive resort in Negril, Jamaica. The rooms were large. There were no doors. The view from Tommy and Alicia's room was breathtaking. They could see both the huge pool and the ocean. They noticed that people were walking around the pool naked. Everyone was free, doing what they wanted to do.

"This is the life," Tommy said.

"I tell you what, it's damn sure different," Alicia said.

Tommy stripped to his boxer shorts. "Take off your clothes, baby. Let's meet Twin and Jennifer at the pool."

"Damn, Tommy. The way you stripped, it's like you've been here before. I'm comfortable with mine, too, but I don't know if I want everybody to see me."

"Everybody is naked. Don't worry about this. I mean, this is what life is all about. You can't take nothing serious. You're born; you grow; you get old; and you die. We have to live every moment. You know what I mean?"

"I guess it's different 'cause you're a man."

"I don't think Jennifer is going to have a problem with being nude, either."

Alicia frowned. "Of course not. She's a stripper."

"Okay, why don't you just come down to the pool in a thong."

"Okay, that might work. And if I get comfortable, I'll take it all off."

*****

At the pool, drinks and roasted duck were being served Tommy and Twin were walking around trying to check out the women. Alicia and Jennifer were relaxing on towels, taking in the sun.

"I'm glad we finally get to talk," Jennifer said. "I feel like I know you from somewhere … your face."

"I heard a lot about you, but you don't look familiar."

"All good, I hope," Jennifer smiled.

Alicia didn't respond.

"Have you ever been to a nude beach before?"

"No."

"Twin tells me that you're from Cali… Don't they have nude beaches in Cali?"

"I think so, but this really isn't my cup of tea."

"Your body is absolutely amazing. I mean, if I had a body like yours … I'd flaunt it."

"Thank you," Alicia said.

"I hope you don't think I'm trying to hit on you."

Alicia laughed a little. "Not at all."

"So how do you feel about the lifestyle?"

"What are you talking about?"

"The lifestyle of being a drug dealer's girl."

"I don't see myself as a drug dealer's girl; I'm just doing my thing, you know? I don't need anything Tommy has. I've always had money."

"Is that so?"

"Yeah. My dad is a real estate mogul."

"I'm from a trailer park, myself."

A waitress appeared. A tall Jamaican man with short dreadlocks. He was holding two drinks. "Two sex on the beaches, compliments of the man sitting at the table on the other side of the pool."

The man stood. He was a white man wearing nothing but a straw hat. His little pink pecker was pointing in their direction.

The women held the drinks up and thanked the man.

"Not my type," Alicia said.

"Definitely not mine," Jennifer said.

"The waiter, though … I'd like to see him if I wasn't involved. You know?"

"Hell yeah. That man is fine," Jennifer said.

"You're cool."

Jennifer became silent. She didn't know what to make of Alicia. She seemed like a girl she could confide in, but she was Tommy's girlfriend. She knew that eventually Tommy would get caught, but she didn't want someone so innocent to go down with him. She hoped that Alicia wasn't holding drugs or money for Tommy. She didn't want her new friend to get in any trouble. "You know the game ain't kind to nobody," Jennifer said.

Alicia looked at Jennifer then said, "I don't know what you're talking about. I'm not breaking any laws. I don't hold drugs. I don't smuggle drugs. I don't take drugs, or dealers' money, or none of that shit."

"So why are you here, and who do you think paid for this trip?"

Alicia was quiet for a minute. Then she sipped her drink. "Good point."

Jennifer got up and walked to the pool. She stuck one foot in. "The water is cold."

"You have a great body yourself."

"Thanks, but you know the tits are store-bought."

"I ain't mad at ya."

"You're cool. I want to tell you something, but I don't know if you can keep a secret."

Their eyes locked.

Twin walked up and smiled.

CHAPTER 25

The sky was blood red as the sun began to fade away. Alicia was lying on the beach in a white G-string. Her head rested on Tommy's lap. He was staring at the sky. She asked what was wrong.

"Oh, nothing."

"Baby, I know you by now. I can tell when something is troubling you."

He smiled. It felt good to have someone who knew him.

"So are you going to tell me?"

"You ever been scared that things are not going to work out the way you planned?"

"What do you mean? Everything is going just fine."

He sighed. "I don't know about that. I feel something just ain't right. You know what I mean?"

She sat up and looked him in his eyes. "Baby, you can't think like that. You gotta think positive. You're a good person, good will always prevail."

"Only in movies. I mean, what you are saying sounds like a Hallmark card. You know?"

"Tommy, like I said, this country was built on lies and deception. Some of the people here with the most wealth have stolen to get it. Don't worry about nothing. You're about to be totally legit."

"You're right. A lot of people have stolen to get ahead, and a lot of people today have beat the system, but most have one thing going for them."

"What's that?" Alicia asked, picking up a handful of sand and then dropping it between her toes.

"Most of them are white. Let me tell you, the white man makes the law. He enforces and interprets the law the way he feels. I just don't think I'm going to make it. I just got a gut feeling that this whole thing is going to come to an end."

Alicia rubbed Tommy's chest. "Baby, you gotta think positive."

Tommy was glad that she was so enthusiastic. He felt good to have her with him, and he started to think positive again.

He leaned forward and kissed her.

"What was that for?"

"Just 'cause I love you. That's all."

"That's so sweet."

The sun had gone down, and a gentle breeze was blowing. Tommy wished the moment could last forever. But he would be handling a transaction in Miami as early as tomorrow.

*****

Morgan and Jennifer sat in the Miami hotel room, prepping the drugs for delivery. The ecstasy was being shrink-wrapped then stuffed into cereal boxes. They prepped the drugs for two hours before Jennifer excused herself to the bathroom.

In the bathroom, she stuffed a hundred X pills into three balloons. *Nobody will know*, she told herself. Out of thousands of pills, who would miss a hundred? There were simply too many for anybody to notice.

When she stepped back into the room, Morgan was finishing the packaging of the product. After they were done, they cleaned the room up really well and made sure that they hadn't dropped any product.

Morgan had rented a dark blue Chrysler 300 from Hertz, but when they were all packed up and ready to drive off, Jennifer made an announcement to Morgan.

"I don't think I can go through with this."

"Why?"

"I don't know. I just feel like something is going to happen."

Morgan looked at her, puzzled. "What? Are you crazy? Nothing is going to happen to us. I mean, we've done this twelve times, and nothing has happened to us."

"Maybe God was on our side. Maybe it was just luck. I don't know," Jennifer said, avoiding Morgan's eyes.

Morgan sighed. "Jennifer, I don't know about you, but I need the money, hon, and I'm willing to chance it."

Jennifer jumped out of the car and opened the trunk.

"What are you doing?" Morgan asked.

"I'm getting my luggage out. I'm catching a flight back to Charlotte."

"Jennifer, you can't leave me."

Jennifer got her suitcase from the trunk and placed it on the pavement.

"I'm calling Twin," Morgan said. She pulled out her cell phone and called Twin.

"Yeah, what up?"

"Jennifer says she not going back with me."

"What the fuck you mean?"

"She says she don't want to do it anymore."

"Let me speak to her."

Morgan passed Jennifer the phone.

"Hello."

"What the fuck is Morgan talking about?"

"I just don't want to do it anymore," Jennifer said.

"Where are you at now?"

"I'm in front of the hotel."

"Okay. Me and Tommy are on our way there. Just hold up another three or four minutes."

Jennifer grabbed a red overnight bag, picked up her suitcase, and walked into the hotel lobby.

Six minutes later, Twin and Tommy entered the lobby.

Jennifer had already asked a bellman to get her a taxi to the airport.

Twin yanked her by the arm and pulled her aside. "What the fuck do you think you are doing?"

"Let go of my fucking arm or I will fucking tell everything I know."

Twin pulled her outside. "I don't know what the fuck you're trying to prove, but you ain't fucking bailing out on me now."

Tommy walked outside but remained silent.

Tears filled Jennifer's eyes. "My heart ain't in this no more, Twin. I just can't go on like this."

"Bitch, you owe me. You do know that you ran off with my money, don't you?"

"I know, and I'm sorry."

"You're damn right you're sorry, but you ain't getting away like this. I will fucking kill you, bitch. Don't you know that after this we won't have to do this shit again?"

"I can't do it. I'm sorry."

"You are going to do it or else ... What the fuck you mean you can't do it? I ain't listening to that shit."

"Don't you ever threaten me. I know your secrets, Twin. I know you set your friends up to get robbed, remember?"

Twin yanked her arm again, this time pulling her so close that she could smell his breath. "I will bring cannons to destroy that trailer park you're from. You hear me?"

"Let me go, Twin, or I swear I will make it bad for your black ass!"

"My black ass? Where the fuck did that come from? You racist little bitch."

"Muthafucka, you know I ain't racist. I been putting up with your ass for years."

The taxi pulled up. The bellman stepped outside with Jennifer's luggage. "Madam, your taxi is here."

Twin let her arm go.

She walked over to the bellman and tipped him.

Jennifer and Twin stared at one another.

The taxi driver finally asked, "Ma'am, are you going to the airport now or later?"

"Goodbye, Twin, and good luck to you."

*****

Jennifer called Mark. He answered on the first ring. "Hey, Mark."

"What's up?"

"Nothing, just leaving Miami. I'm sure you know that already."

"What do you mean?"

"You know, the girl whose picture is on your dresser, muthafucka."

"What are you talking about?"

"Mark, I slept at your house. I put two and two together. Now come off the bullshit."

He hesitated. "So, does Tommy and Twin know what you know?"

"No. Nobody knows shit."

"So, you decided not to come back with Morgan, huh?"

"You know everything, huh?"

"I'm a fed, remember?"

"Yeah, I decided not to come back with Morgan."

"That was a good choice, because it's going to go down soon, you know."

"You were going to bust me, huh?"

He sighed. "I had no choice; I mean, it's business, not personal."

"Yeah, but I helped you, muthafucka. I gave you information, and I've fucked you, Mark. Remember the shit you said about me getting my life together? Was that all part of your fuckin games?"

"No. I would never play with you like that. Listen, you're getting emotional."

"Oh, is that what I am?"

Flight 355 to Charlotte, North Carolina is now boarding.

"Well I have a plane to catch, Agent Pratt." Jennifer ended the call.

She sat on row 25-A in a window seat. Nobody had the middle seat, but an elderly white man had the aisle seat. Jennifer thought about Twin, Tommy, and JoJo, and how their lives were about to be destroyed simply because they wanted to better their financial situations. She thought about Tommy in particular, though Twin was once her man. Tommy had been used by everybody around him. Then she thought about Mark again. She thought he had been genuinely interested in her well-being, but he'd used her for personal gain. How could she be so stupid? How could she fall for the police? Tears rolled down her face. She felt so used.

She pulled a cell phone from her purse and decided to make one more call. She would call Twin to tell him what was going on—not because she wanted to save his ass, but because she wanted to spare Tommy. He was really a good person. She dialed Twin's number.

No answer.

She tried again, but still no answer.

The flight attendant announced that all cell phones had to be turned off at this time.

She dialed Twin's number one last time and ducked behind the seats.

Twin answered. "Listen, you dirty bitch, I wish you quit calling my phone."

"I got to tell you something."

A flight attendant walked over. The thin black woman with short hair said, "Ma'am turn off your cell phone."

"Twin, listen to me."

"Ma'am, turn off your cell phone or else I'll have to ask you to exit the plane," the flight attendant said again.

"Listen, man..." Jennifer pleads.

"Eat shit and die, bitch," Twin said and ended the call.

Jennifer looked up at the flight attendant, smiled, and turned the cell phone off.

Five minutes later, the plane took off.

She dozed, her head resting against the window.

CHAPTER 26

An hour later, when the plane arrived in Charlotte, the old man sitting next to Jennifer shook her. "Hey, it's time to get off the plane. We're here."

Jennifer didn't move, so the man shook her again, but still there was no response. He called the flight attendant.

The woman with the short hair came, and an older blonde woman with a nametag that read: 'Peggy' took Jennifer's pulse. "Oh my God! She has no pulse. Somebody get a doctor."

A tall white man with graying hair announced that he was a doctor. Everybody made room for the man. He loosened his tie and checked for Jennifer's pulse. Nothing. He checked her heart. No sign of a heartbeat. The man tilted Jennifer's head back and performed CPR, but she still did not breathe.

The captain came to the back where everybody was staring.

The doctor looked into the captain's eyes and announced, "I'm afraid she's dead."

"Oh no," Peggy said.

"My guess is that she has been dead for at least ten minutes," the doctor said.

*****

Twin had just arrived in Charlotte when he got the call from Barb, Jennifer's mother. When he saw the number on the caller ID, he was inclined to ignore the call, but then decided that it would be best to advise her not to call him again. "Hello."

"You black muthafucka. I know you killed my daughter."

"What are you talking about? Nobody's dead, stupid bitch."

"Jennifer's gone, and I know you had something to do with it."

"Who told you that?"

"The hospital called me today and said she had died on a plane from Miami, and I know that's where you took her."

"Are you serious? This is no time to be playing games, woman."

"Do you think I would play games with you like that ... about my daughter, my flesh and blood?"

"How did she die?" Twin asked. He began to feel emotional.

"You killed her. That's how she died, and that's what I'm going to tell the police, and that's what I'm going to tell the hospital ... that your sorry ass killed her."

Twin moved the phone away from his ear as Barbara kept shouting obscenities. Finally he hung up. He called Tommy.

"Hello."

"Jennifer died."

"What are you talking about?"

"Her Mom just called me and told me she died on the plane from Miami."

"Are you serious?"

"That's what the bitch said."

Tommy sighed. "I wonder do Morgan know."

"She couldn't know. She's still on the road."

"Have you checked on her to make sure she hasn't been pulled over or anything?"

"No, but I'm going to call her in a minute."

"Don't tell her about Jennifer just yet. You know how women can get all emotional and shit."

"Yeah, you're right. I'll talk to you later," Twin said and hung up the phone. He began to pace. He thought about Jennifer and what she had meant to him. He thought about the good times they'd had in the beginning of their relationship. He felt like they were meant for one another. Although she was white, she could identify with his struggle. She was an outcast, too. Her family was poor, as was his; and she had an occupation that people frowned upon. So did he.

He picked up a picture of Jennifer and himself taken at an amusement park. They were so happy then. He remembered all the stares he would get from black women, but he didn't care. He was with someone who truly understood him, regardless of color, and he believed that Jennifer truly loved him. That was before the big money, the trips to Miami, and the kilos of cocaine ... before Tommy got the major connection with Manny.

He'd always hustled, but never on a major level. He was considered small-time when he met Jennifer, selling an ounce of cocaine here and there to supplement his income. He had been a city sanitation worker, but he always dressed nice and drove nice cars, so women always thought he was a big-time hustler.

The money came, and so did the problems. Jennifer would complain that they weren't spending enough time together. So he'd give her money to keep her mouth shut. He'd buy her new purses and jewels to make up for lost time together. And then it was new cars, and he'd even given her the money to buy her new breasts. This kept her quiet for a few weeks, but then she wanted to go to Miami. Twin had initially told her that she couldn't come, but she was adamant, even accused him of seeing "some bitch" in Miami. After weeks of opposition, Twin finally let her come. She became part of the operation. Jennifer became a drug-trafficking mule. The money had changed Twin, had changed his relationship, and had replaced the love of his life. He'd gotten to the point where he needed then money more than Jennifer.

Twin picked up another picture of Jennifer. She was smiling brightly. It was her 25th birthday. He kissed the picture, and the tears continued to fall.

*****

Twin hopped in his truck and drove to JoJo's house.

Nia answered the door. She invited him in.

"What's up, Twin? Why you look so down?" JoJo asked.

"Jennifer died."

"What?" JoJo said. "Come in and have a seat."

They sat in the living room. Nia stood beside Joe. Nobody said anything for about a minute. Finally JoJo asked, "How did she die?"

"I don't know. All I know so far is that she passed out on the plane."

"I'm sorry to hear that."

"Yeah, I know. This whole thing has made me realize that life is too short, and I think you and Tommy should try to work out your differences. We've been friends for too long."

"I'm willing to put all the bullshit behind us," JoJo said.

Twin sighed, then he glanced at Nia.

"Hey, Twin, I'm sorry Tommy had to get hurt ... I really am. I mean, we all know Tommy's a good person. The man wears his heart on his sleeve, and we know there's nothing he won't do for anybody," Nia said.

"I know, and that's what's fucked up about the whole situation," Twin said. "Even though Tommy said he was thinking of moving to San Fran with Alicia, we don't want him holding a grudge."

"You're right, I think I should call and talk to him first," Nia said.

"I think I should talk to him first," JoJo said.

Twin stood. "I have to be going. I have to find out what happened to Jennifer."

JoJo and Twin hugged.

*****

A task force comprised of state and local police and the DEA, was waiting along the Little Rock Road exit, looking out for a blue Chrysler 300, with a white female driver.

Mark Pratt, received a call. "Hello. Pratt speaking."

"This is vice detective, Brad Thomas."

"How's it going, Brad? Haven't heard from you in a while."

"Yeah, I know, almost a year."

"What's up?"

"Bad news."

"What's wrong?"

"One of your informants died. OD'd off X. Balloons filled with X were discovered in her stomach."

Ken Clarkson walked over. "What's going on, Mark?"

"Who?"

"Paige Howard."

"Oh no!" Mark said.

"Yeah. She died on a plane inbound from Miami."

"Dammit, man. That's bad!" Mark said, sniffling. "How do they know she OD'd?"

"What's going on, Mark?" Ken Clarkson asked again.

"Paige died."

"How? When?"

"Yesterday. She was obviously smuggling X. It was found in her system."

"X?"

"Yeah. She died on a plane."

"Do you think her boyfriend put her up to bringing the X back on the plane?"

"I don't know. Anything's possible. Remember the time he had her call in and give us a tip on the two girls so Paige could smuggle the coke successfully?"

"Yeah. The guy is a real winner," Ken said sarcastically.

A uniformed cop approached Mark and Ken. "A Chrysler 300 has been spotted about two miles away."

"Hopefully, Morgan will have all the answers," Mark said.

*****

A state trooper in a blue Mustang pulled Morgan over. She looked at the man in disbelief when he told her she was swerving.

"License and registration please."

"This is a rental."

"Okay. Where is the rental agreement?"

Morgan opened the glove compartment but found no rental agreement. She checked the console but still no sign of an agreement.

"Hey, listen; I don't know where the agreement is, but here is my license," Morgan said, handing the man her license.

The tall trooper looked at the license, passed it back to Morgan, and asked, "Ma'am, would you step out of the car?"

Morgan looked as if she was about to cry. "Sir, what the hell is going on?"

A second trooper pulled up beside them, then an unmarked car pulled up. Mark Pratt and Ken Clarkson presented their badges.

Morgan started crying. "I don't understand what's going on?"

"Ma'am, we have reason to believe that you are trafficking ecstasy."

"Somebody lied on me. I don't know what you're talking about."

"Why are you crying?" Clarkson asked.

"Because you're just picking on me."

"Do you mind if we search your car?" Mark asked.

"Hell no, I don't want you to search my car."

Ken opened the car door, popped the trunk, and searched two suitcases before finding an overnight bag. He dumped the contents on the ground. Thousands of pills covered the ground. "Let me guess:

You have a headache and this is your medicine," Ken said.

"Fuck you!"

"No, fuck *you*. We're going to put you away for a long time." Ken laughed.

Mark ordered the trooper to cuff Morgan.

Tears filled her eyes. "Don't take me to jail. Please don't take me."

"It's too late for that," Ken said.

"Take the cuffs off her," Mark requested. "Morgan, take a walk with me."

*****

Inside the red SUV, Mark and Morgan sat and talked. She told him how she started dancing after she left home. Morgan was from Connecticut and had attended community college but never completed school. She went to work at Hooters for two years and made good money, but was told that the real money was in exotic dancing; so she started dancing at Twin Peaks. Most of the patrons were rednecks and Mexicans with very little money. She found her home in the Uptown Carousel. It was a clean club and most of the girls were very pretty, and this brought the elite clientele—athletes, businessmen and, of course, the hustlers—all of whom had money to throw away. She had taken a liking to Paige because Paige had showed her the ropes, the ins and outs of the club, the customers with the money, and the ones who didn't have. Morgan broke down into tears when Mark told her that Paige had died.

"You're lying. Please tell me you're lying."

"I'm afraid not. I wish it weren't true, but she died on the plane. They found X in her system."

"What?" Morgan looked surprised.

"Yeah, they found X in her system. She had swallowed three balloons filled with pills."

Morgan's face was the color of a tomato. Her eyes were puffy. She couldn't control her crying.

Mark hugged her then said, "Morgan, it's too late for Paige, but it isn't too late for you."

"What do you mean?"

"I need you to help us bring Tommy, Twin, and JoJo down. They are the bad guys. You hear me?"

Morgan looked Mark in his eyes. "Yeah, they are the bad guys."

"Now, I'm going to need you to get one of them on the phone and tell them that everything is okay, and that you want to deliver the goods."

"I can't do that."

"Why can't you do that?"

"I don't want to get anybody in trouble."

"Listen. Your friend is dead because of these guys."

Morgan wiped her face then looked out the window of the SUV. "I can't do it."

"What do you mean? It's your life here. Do you know there was a girl who got busted last week with five pills and got a year for each pill? You have thousands of pills and only one life."

"I understand what you're saying, but I can't do it. I'll just have to get my dad to get me a good lawyer."

"This case is federal. There's nothing a good lawyer can do for you."

"I made my bed. I'm going to have to lie in it."

"Are you sure you know what you're talking about?"

She thought about it. And thought about it. She wasn't sure at all. She would have to think long and hard about it on the way to the federal building.

CHAPTER 27

"Hello."

"Hey, Tommy, everything is okay," Morgan said.

"How far are you away?"

"About three hours."

"Three hours? You should be here by now. Are you sure everything is okay?"

"Yeah, Tommy everything is fine."

"Are you calling me from your cell phone?"

"Yes," Morgan said.

"Your number never came up private before."

"Tommy, would you like for me to call you again?"

"No. I'm just wondering."

"Hey, Tommy, did you hear what happened to Jenny?" Morgan said, trying to change the subject.

"No. What happened?"

"She died on the plane."

"How do you know?"

"Her family called me and told me."

"Damn, that's a tragedy."

"I hear that they found X in her system."

"Is that right?"

"Yeah, she would often steal X from you guys."

"Why are you talking like that?"

"Like what?"

"Talking about drugs and shit. I don't fuck with no X."

"I'm sorry."

"Hey, Morgan, you aint sounding right; is the cops with you?"

"Hell no!"

"Call me back; I want to see your number on my caller ID." Tommy hung up the phone."

Morgan turned to Ken and Mark. "Where is my cell phone?"

"It's with the evidence."

"Can you get it? He's suspicious."

"Yeah, he's smart."

It took Ken five minutes to get Morgan's cell phone. When he entered the interrogation room, he handed it to her and she called Tommy again.

"Hello."

"Did my number show up this time?"

"Yeah, I guess you must have been in a bad area."

"Yeah, okay, like I was saying, where do you want me to come see you?"

"I don't know; I'll call you back with that?" Tommy said then hung up the phone.

*****

JoJo's number appeared on Tommy's cell phone. *What the fuck does this nigga want? I done told his punk ass I don't want to have nothing to do with him.* Tommy pushed the button to send him to voice mail.

JoJo called again.

This time Tommy answered. "Yeah, what do you want? I don't fuck with you; Twin handles your side of the business."

"I want to talk."

"About what?"

"I want to talk about us, man. You know we've been friends too long to be at odds with each other over some bullshit."

"Okay, stealing my woman is some bullshit?"

"Tommy, you want Nia to be faithful to you, but have you been faithful to her?"

"That's beside the point." Tommy hung the phone up.

JoJo called again.

"Hello."

"Tommy, did you know that Jenny died?"

"Yeah, I know she died."

"Man, we need to at least be on speaking terms before something bad happens to one of us."

"Joe, man, this is it. After the packgage makes it, I'm off to Cali.

You can stay here with your *wife*. You got her, buddy."

"Tommy—"

Tommy hung up the phone.

*****

Alicia called Tommy but he sent her to voicemail. There was simply too much going on right now to be somewhere cuddled up with her. A white woman had died—of an overdose of ecstasy. Ecstasy that he'd paid for with his own money. He figured the feds were probably checking her phone records to see whom she'd been in contact with. Hell, they knew she was Twin's girlfriend. There was nothing good that could possibly come out of that. Tommy went home and changed his clothes. He wanted to go somewhere to think; he needed solitude. He wanted to go to the lake but decided against it when Twin showed up at his house.

"What's up, Twin?"

"Nothing, man." Twin began to pace.

Tommy could tell that there was a lot on his mind.

"I'm just so fucked up, man. You know I just can't believe that my baby is gone."

"I know, right? I don't know what to do, either. I mean, the other white chick called me. She was acting real weird, saying shit she shouldn't have been saying on the phone."

"Shit like what."

"Suggesting that Jennifer stole some X from us."

Twin's face became serious. "Do you think she's been busted?"

"I don't know, but she's claiming she's going to be here in three hours."

"She should have been here by now."

"I know. That's why I don't know about meeting her. She knows about Jenny."

"How did she know that?"

"Says Jenny's family called her."

Twin sat on Tommy's sofa. "Well, there is no way for me to check that because her stupid-ass mom won't talk to me."

*****

Tommy was about to get in his car when someone called out his name. When he turned to see who was calling him, he recognized the man immediately. It was J-Black, the man who'd robbed him twice.

J-Black was smiling and holding a chrome handgun.

Tommy took a step back, still watching the gun.

"Let's go back upstairs."

"Hey, man, I aint got no drugs or money."

"Nigga, don't tell me what you ain't got; just take me upstairs."

Once inside the apartment, J-Black ordered Tommy to stand to the side with his hands on his head. "If you take your hands off your head, I'mma blast your ass."

"I'm telling you, there ain't shit in here."

"Shut the fuck up," J-Black said. He searched Tommy. "Okay, where is it?"

"What are you talking about?"

"The dope, nigga, don't play dumb with me." J-Black cocked the hammer of the handgun.

"Listen, man, don't kill me. I'm telling you the truth; there ain't shit here."

A sudden hardness appeared on J-Black's face. "Okay, where is that punk ass Twin? I know that coward done moved or something."

"I don't know where Twin is."

"Oh, you trying to take up for this nigga? This is the same nigga that told me where the fuck you lived."

"What are you talking about?"

"The first time I robbed your bitch ass for those bricks."

"What about it?"

"Twin put me up on that, and we split the dough."

"I don't believe that."

J-Black chuckled. "You're a simple-minded nigga. Just think about it. First I rob you, then I rob your boy's sister's house, then I rob you again and nobody had ever robbed Twin. Why do you think this is so?"

Tommy couldn't concentrate for a moment.

"So where the fuck is Twin?"

"I don't know."

J-Black placed the gun to Tommy's temple.

Tommy's cell phone rang. "I need to answer my phone."

J-Black gritted his teeth. "No, nigga, you need to answer *me*. Where the fuck is Twin?"

Tommy felt the cold steel against his head. His whole life flashed before him—peewee football games, elementary school parties, high school dances, his mother's funeral.

"I'mma count to three; if you ain't told me where I can find Twin, I'm going to blow your fucking block off."

"Hey, I don't know but I can find out," Tommy said anxious to punish Twin himself.

J-Black lowered the gun.

Tommy called Twin on his cell phone.

Twin answered on the first ring. "Yo, nigga, I've been trying to call you."

"Yeah, what's up?"

"On the news they are saying that Paige was suspected of being part of a large drug trafficking ring."

"Shit."

"Tommy, I called a minute ago to see if my wallet came out of my pocket when I was sitting on your sofa."

"Yeah, it did. I can bring it to you where are you staying?"

"The Holiday Inn, Carowinds Boulevard. Room 417."

"I'll be over in twenty minutes."

*****

Twin opened the door and flinched when he saw J-Black pointing a nine-millimeter at his head.

"What are you doing here?"

"I'm here for what's mine."

"How did you find out I was here?"

"You got some really good friends."

"What are you talking about?"

"I guess old Fatboy must've decided to give you up, since you gave him up." J-Black shoved Twin inside and closed the door behind him. "Nigga, put your hands on your head."

Twin complied.

"I need some money and I need it fast."

"I ain't got shit."

J-Black slapped Twin with the butt of the gun.

Twin fell on the sofa holding his head. "I ain't got shit, Black, I swear to you."

J-Black stuck the barrel of the handgun in Twin's mouth. "Pretend you're sucking a dick, nigga."

Twin gagged.

J-Black pulled the gun from Twin's mouth.

Twin gasped for air.

"I want you to lick this gun like you're licking the shaft of a dick, or else I'mma blow your fucking brains out."

"I ain't doing that shit."

J-Black cocked the hammer back, turned his head sideways, and aimed. "You ain't gonna do what?"

Twin stuck his tongue out then started licking the gun.

J-Black smiled. "Now that's what I'm talking about, pussy-ass nigga."

Twin's saliva covered the barrel.

J-Black unzipped his pants and began to stroke himself.

Twin stopped. "This shit is disgusting. What are you, some kind of homo?"

"Keep licking the gun or else ..."

"I can't do it. You'll just have to shoot me and hope nobody at this hotel hears the shot."

J-Black pulled the trigger.

The bullet entered the center of Twin's face and tore through the back of his head. He was lifeless by the time he crashed face down on the floor.

J-Black began to feel nauseous when he saw Twin's brain bits on the wall. He zipped his pants up. He hated the fact that Twin had provoked him. There was no time to search the hotel room. It was time to go.

CHAPTER 28

The next day, Tommy was at the lake. He'd taken only the pole his mother had bought him. The first pole. He was sitting on the bank with his shoes off, like he had done when he was a little kid, listening to the crickets. He thought about all then money he'd made in the drug trade and how he was still unhappy. It seemed the more money he'd made the more complex his life had become, and he still couldn't find happiness. No matter how many women he slept with or how expensive the car, something was still missing. Something that money couldn't buy.

He thought about what Alicia had said about most rich people having gotten their money from ill gains. The people that run this country had even stolen. America was built on thievery. The country itself had been stolen, taken from the Indians. He considered the fact that rappers were usually presenting an image to Black America on how to live, images of black men being players and black women being whores. An image that he himself had bought into. *I just had to have a Maybach, a three hundred thousand dollar car.* He got more enjoyment out of casting his line into the lake than driving the car.

How in the hell could I be so stupid? How could I let greed consume me? How could I let American culture get the best of me?

He felt a tugging on his line. He pulled the small brim out of the water then tossed it back. When he looked up he saw Alicia.

She smiled at him. "I figured you would be here."

"Is that right?" He said as he stood and looked at her with concern. "What's wrong, baby?"

"It's just way too much shit going on. I mean, the white girl overdosed; the feds are saying she's part of a drug trafficking ring. Alicia, I think my days are numbered, you know what I mean?"

She looked sad. "Don't say that."

"Hey, and now I have to decide if I want to meet this other white girl to get the X she's bringing back from Miami."

"Why wouldn't you want to meet her? This is supposed to be the last trip, isn't it?"

"Yeah."

She put her head on his chest and held his hand tightly.

"What do you think I should do?"

She looked at him. "I think you should go meet the white girl, get your product, and go ahead with the plans."

"I thought you were ... always anti-drug."

"I know, but you made your plan, so stick to it."

"I still got a funny feeling about the whole situation."

*****

As soon as Tommy stepped inside his apartment, JoJo called. He sent him to voicemail. Another call soon followed from a number that Tommy had never seen. He answered, hoping it wasn't JoJo. "Hello. Hello."

A woman was crying. "My baby is gone ... My baby is gone."

"Who is this?"

"This is Ms. Sarah, Twin's mother."

"Hey, Ms. Sarah. What's wrong?"

"My baby has been found dead."

Tommy's heart sank. He'd known J-Black was going to pay Twin a little visit, maybe extort him a little bit, but, damn. He couldn't believe J-Black had actually killed him. "Please tell me you're lying, Ms. Sarah."

She started crying again. "I wouldn't ever lie about a thing like that; this is no time to play."

"What happened?"

"That's what I was calling you for, to find out what happened. You're around him a lot more than I am."

"I don't know what happened, Ms. Sarah. I saw him earlier today, but that was it. I hadn't been around him much today."

"Did he owe somebody some money or something? His brother said it was probably a drug debt."

"I don't think so."

"I heard that white girl died on the plane; do you think her family killed my baby?"

Tommy was silent. Tears filled his eyes. He thought about his mother and how she would have felt if he had been killed. He was hurt for Ms. Sarah. He knew he had played a major part in the death.

"Do you think that trailer trash white girl's family had something to do with my baby getting killed?"

"I don't know, Ms. Sarah."

"I need you to come see me, baby. I've been looking at pictures all day, and I was looking at the one of you and the twins at Easter when y'all was about ten, the ones y'all took when you wore the sailor suits."

Tommy smiled. "Yeah, I remember."

"Yeah, y'all was so cute. You was always such a chubby kid, much heavier than the twins."

"Yeah, I was always *Fatboy*."

"Tommy, I want you to come over to my house, baby. There will be plenty to eat, and we're just going to celebrate my son's life."

"I promise to come see you, Ms. Sarah."

*****

Morgan's number appeared on the caller ID again. Tommy answered the phone.

"So what you gonna do, Tommy? I've been calling you for the past twenty-four hours now."

"What do you mean?"

"I have your product, remember? I've been back since yesterday but you—"

"No, I don't remember, but you remember me hanging up on your ass before, don't you?"

"Are we going to meet or what?"

"Right now, I got too much on my mind. Twin has been murdered, you know?"

"Murdered?"

"Yeah. He was found dead in a hotel room."

"Wow! I'm sorry to hear that."

Tommy took a deep breath. "Yeah, I got a lot going on."

"Tommy, I know you got a lot going on, but I'm getting nervous, man."

"Why?"

"The news is saying that Jennifer is suspected of being part of a drug ring."

"That has nothing to do with you."

"I know, Tommy ... I don't want no part of this shit no more. I think I'm going to flush these pills; they're the reason for all this shit happening."

"No, you can't do that."

"But, Tommy, I'm scared."

"Everything is going to be okay. Whatever you do, don't get rid of my shit! You hear me?"

"Okay, Tommy, you don't have to shout." Morgan was now calm again.

"Listen, let me go to see Twin's mom, and then I'll meet you. No ... matter of fact, we'll hook up tomorrow because ain't no telling how long I'll be at Twin's house."

*****

Mark Pratt had convinced the Magistrate to let Morgan out on her own recognizance. He conveyed the fact that she was being very cooperative in an ongoing investigation. Before Morgan was released, Mark told her how important it was that she kept in contact with him. He told her to tell him if Tommy calls again and wants to meet immediately. A sting operation with the local task force could be set up quickly.

*****

"I got immediate release," J.C. said to Tommy over the phone.

"Where are you now?"

"I'm at a little bus station about five miles away from the prison."

"Do you need me to come and get you?"

"No, I can catch the bus. I should be there around eight tonight."

"I got something to tell you."

"What's wrong, Son? You sound sad."

"Yeah, Twin got killed."

"Oh my God, Son. I'm sorry to hear that."

"Yeah, they are going to bury him in a few days."

"You going?"

204

"Naw, I ain't going. I might go view the body."

"My God ... Son, I'm sorry to hear that; I know he was your friend."

"Yeah, I'm a little fucked up behind it."

"But how is everything else going?"

"Everything has been going fucked up, to be honest with you. I'll just wait to tell you when I see you in person."

"Well come pick me up at the Greyhound bus station at eight o'clock."

"Okay."

CHAPTER 29

Tommy was in his Porsche truck, on his way to Alicia's place. He decided to call Don to fill him in on what was going on. The Mercedes dealership had just repossessed the Maybach. He dialed Don's number and an automated recording revealed that the number was no longer in service. Tommy looked at the number then dialed it again, reaching the same message. He immediately dialed Alicia's number. Her number was out of service, too.

He arrived at her apartment and knocked on the door.

A neighbor walked over. A small white lady with freckles and thick glasses. "I think she moved out yesterday."

Tommy looked puzzled. "What do you mean, *moved out*?

"I saw a big moving truck outside and a couple of guys taking all of her stuff out."

"Did you find out where she was going?"

"Didn't think to ask. I really didn't know her; we just kind of spoke here and there in passing."

Tommy walked off without thanking the lady. He got back in his truck and drove aimlessly. He was just trying to take it all in. Alicia was gone and nobody knew where the hell she was. Her phone was disconnected; her dad's phone was disconnected; and he had $750,000 of Tommy's. He called Alicia's school and asked for admissions. "I need to know if you have an Alicia Anderson still enrolled."

"Hold on a second, I'll take a look," a voice on the other end said.

Tommy held onto the phone, fuming. He wondered what the hell was going on. He wondered whether he would get his money back. For the first time, he felt as though Alicia and her father might have been crooks. He was hoping he was wrong.

The woman came back on the phone. "Sir, are you still there?"

"Yeah."

"I searched all my records and I don't have an Alicia Anderson."

"Are you sure?"

"Positive."

"What the hell is going on?" Tommy said.

"Sir, why are you cursing?"

"I'm sorry. I was just thinking out loud." He terminated the call. His mind drifted back to their first conversation about money. *Most people steal somehow or another. My understanding is that very few get it honestly.*

*****

Tommy met his dad with a big hug. "Man, I'm glad to see you on the other side of the fence," Tommy said.

"He'll, I'm glad to be back."

"Let's get in the car and ride. I have some things I need to tell you."

When they were in the car, Tommy fired up the ignition and turned to his father. "Dad, I think I've been robbed."

"Somebody broke into your house?"

"Not that kind of robbed. You remember the girl I was telling you about, the fine one from California?"

"Yeah, you said you were investing your money with her dad."

Tommy looked in his father's direction but avoided his eyes.

"Come on with it, son, what happened?"

"I think I've been had."

"What do you mean?"

Tommy made eye contact with J.C. "Well, I gave her dad $750,000 and now I can't find him."

J.C. was speechless for a moment, then he said, "Pull this muthafucka over right now."

Tommy pulled over to the side of the road.

"Nigga, how in the hell can you give a muthafucka that much money? Do you know that I ain't seen that kind of money in my life?"

Tommy took a deep breath but remained silent.

"Boy, what the hell were you thinking?"

"I don't know, Dad … I don't know. All I know is that I went out to Cali with Alicia, and her dad had all these Benzes and shit like real expensive jewelry. I thought he was legit."

"Oh my God. You still got some money don't you?"

"Only product."

"Only product? Well, you need to get rid of the product and get some money."

"I got one problem."

"What's wrong now?"

"I don't actually have the product. I was supposed to meet the white girl yesterday to get the dope that she brought back from Miami, but then Twin was murdered."

"What does this have to do with you getting your shit?" J.C. ran his fingers through his braids. "I'm not understanding."

"Dad, it's something strange going on with the white girl. I don't know but my gut is telling me not to meet her."

"Well that settles it; don't meet her. What ever you do, don't go meet that girl."

"But I ain't got shit."

"We got each other, and that's all we need."

"I know that but, Daddy, you don't know how I feel," Tommy said as tears rolled down his cheeks.

J.C. turned Tommy's face toward him. "Now you gonna stop all that whining and shit. You gotta be a man, and money don't make you a man. What makes you a man is what you stand for, and all this shit these niggas did was just to show you that they are coward-asses, including the man that took your money."

J.C. had always had a way of making Tommy feel like everything was going to be okay. Tommy remembered when he'd tried out for basketball in middle school and had gotten cut. He'd cried and cried for three days. J.C. pulled him aside and explained to him that since he was a little overweight, he would probably make a better wrestler. Tommy later tried out for wrestling and made the team. He went on to become the state champion. J.C. had never had anything to give to him, but he had been there for him. He'd taught him how to be a man.

Tommy hugged his father. J.C. whispered in his ear, "Everything is going to be okay."

*****

Mark Pratt met Morgan at *Dean & Duluca* for coffee. They sat in the back.

"So you're the guy that used to meet Jenny here, huh?" Morgan asked.

"How do you figure?"

Morgan played with her hair. "Just guessing. She once told me about this fabulous man that she would meet for coffee sometimes."

Mark smiled but didn't say anything.

"This is crazy," Morgan said.

"What's crazy?"

"The fact that Jenny's been on the inside the whole time."

"I wouldn't exactly say she's been on the inside ... more like playing both sides of the fence."

"Is that what you call it? Let me ask you something, Agent Pratt?"

"Go ahead."

She looked him straight in his eyes. "This is kind of a personal question."

"What is it?"

"Do you miss Jenny?"

"Why do you ask that?"

She twirled her hair again, looking innocent. "Just curious."

"I hate that she's gone, if that's what you mean."

She smiled. "That's what I meant."

He sipped his coffee. "I need you to get Tommy, and he'll lead us to JoJo."

"I don't think Tommy and JoJo are speaking now."

"They aren't. I know this."

"Damn, you know everything. How did you know this?"

"Telephones. They can be your best friend or your worst enemy."

"Okay, I'm going to need you to wear a wire."

"A wire?"

"Yeah. I'm going to need to have his voice recorded during the transaction."

"Couldn't you just bust him when I deliver him the drugs?"

"Yeah, but we want to make sure the case is airtight."

Morgan stared at Mark then asked, "Do you have a conscience?"

Mark laughed. "Of course I have a conscience. Why do you ask that?"

"Because you're ruining people's lives."

"People are ruining their own lives with the decisions they make. I didn't tell you to traffic drugs; you decided that on your own."

"Agent Pratt, you're a cold-hearted individual."

Mark grabbed his cup of coffee, sipped it, then left.

*****

Tommy picked up his cell phone and noticed that he'd missed four calls. Three calls were from Morgan. He went against his gut feeling and called her.

She answered on the first ring. "Yeah."

"Talk, but watch your language."

"Okay. Tommy, I have something that belongs to you."

Tommy didn't say anything.

"Tommy, are you going to meet me or not?"

"I don't know; let me call you back."

"You know what, Tommy, just forget it. I'm just going to flush them all.

"No!"

"Well, let's meet."

"Let me call you back in five minutes." He ended the call.

JoJo called again. Tommy answered the phone. "Hello."

"Can we talk?"

"We're talking. What do you want?'

"I know this might be a fucked up time to talk about business, with Twin being dead, but we need to put all our differences aside and make some money."

"You know what, Joe? Fuck you and fuck Twin."

"Twin is dead. Why are you talking like that about him?"

"Nigga, Twin was the one having us robbed all the time."

"I don't believe it."

"Like I didn't want to believe you was fuckin Nia."

"Tommy, are you serious?"

"Come on, man listen. I get robbed then you get robbed, but this nigga never got robbed."

"So who told you this?"

"J-Black, the nigga that robbed us."

"Do you think J-Black had something—"

"Let's meet out somewhere."

"Where?"

"Downtown, the parking lot across from the RockBottom Café."

"How long will it take you?"

"Twenty minutes."

*****

Tommy stood in the middle of the parking lot. J.C. was in the car listening to the radio.

JoJo pulled up in his Porsche truck and walked over to Tommy. "What's up?"

Tommy looked around suspiciously.

"What the fuck you all nervous and shit for?" JoJo asked.

"Man, it's the ninth inning; this game is about to be over."

"What is that supposed to mean?"

"Meaning it's over, Joe; the game is over. There is nothing else to do."

"What am I supposed to do about money?"

"Well at least you got some."

Joe looked at Tommy oddly.

"Remember the real estate guy that I was telling you about in Cali?"

"Your girl's father."

"Yeah. He fucked me out of all my dough."

"How?"

"He won't return my phone calls and neither will she. She's moved and I've given this man $750,000 but ain't got shit to show for it."

"What about the product you and Twin went to get in Miami?"

"The white girl keeps calling me to come get it, but I'm just kind of leery, you know? I just don't feel right about it."

"If you decide to go get it, I know somebody who will buy it all, and you can make at least three hundred grand ... it's just a thought. I mean, everybody is wanting the butterflies."

Tommy took a deep breath. "I'll call her later today."

*****

Morgan was surprised when Tommy called her and said that he needed to see her.

"Do you still have that?"

"Yeah, of course I do. Why wouldn't I have it?"

"Well, you said you was going to flush them."

She laughed. "I was kidding and kind of emotional. You know

after what happened to Jenny."

"Yeah, I feel ya."

"Can you meet me at my job, maybe in the parking lot? Then I can go on in to work."

"I'm on my way." He ended the call then pondered for a while. His plan was to get the pills, sell them to JoJo, and take his dad to Atlanta, Georgia or Dallas, Texas to start a new life. Perhaps he would buy a boat so that he and his dad could go fishing in the ocean. He looked up to the sky and said to God, "If you let me get through this situation without going to jail, I promise that I will never knowingly and willingly do anything wrong or illegal." He felt bad after saying that because, though he wasn't a big bible reader, he'd read some-where that you weren't supposed to test the Lord.

CHAPTER 30

Tommy arrived at the Uptown Carousel parking lot and scanned the area. He didn't see anything strange. He'd been in the club a few times so he recognized one of the bouncers from the club standing at the back door.

The man nodded at him but didn't say anything. He then ushered a skinny black stripper through the back door.

Tommy drove to the parking lot across the street. Looking around, nothing seemed out of the ordinary. He jumped out of the car and walked back across the street to the door where the bouncer was standing. "How much tonight, buddy?" He really didn't care how much it cost. He had no intentions of going in the club.

The man said, "Seven dollars for members, ten dollars for non-members."

"Thanks, man." Tommy walked back across the street to sit in the car.

Morgan arrived driving a red Volkswagen Beetle. She got out of the car then looked around the parking lot and across the street before making eye contact with Tommy. She smiled before walking across the street with the gym bag.

She sat on the passenger side of Tommy's car.

"So what you got for me?"

"What you got for *me* is the question?" she asked.

Tommy looked at her with serious eyes. "Can I give you a thousand dollars now? Once I sell some product, I'll give you the rest."

She held her hand out.

Tommy dug into his pocket, pulled out a wad of money, and peeled of ten one- hundred-dollar bills.

The X was in a paper bag inside the gym bag. Tommy took the X from the gym bag.

"Call me when you have the rest of the money."

"I will. Thanks a lot, Morgan."

She got out of the car.

*****

When she got out of the vehicle, she dropped a napkin on the ground, signaling to the feds that the exchange had been made.

Mark Pratt was driving a Toyota Tacoma. He sped across the parking lot and blocked Tommy's truck. Another car, a white Lincoln Continental blocked him from the rear. DEA and task force members soon swarmed the parking lot.

Tommy jumped out of the car.

A huge cop with a red beard chased Tommy and soon caught up with him. The man jumped on Tommy's back but was slung to the ground.

Mark Pratt put the Tacoma in park, jumped out and pointed a handgun. "Stop, Tommy!"

Tommy looked back and kept running.

He was tackled by Ken Clarkson. A fat black DEA agent restrained his arms while placing a knee in his back.

Tommy yelled, "Get the fuck off me!"

Fatso stood Tommy up.

"Bitch set me up!" Tommy said.

"The classic line." Ken laughed. He walked off, anxious to retrieve the drugs.

Tommy looked at Morgan.

She made eye contact briefly but then got in her car and drove away.

Ken came back with a bag of X. "This is a lot of shit."

Tommy didn't say anything.

"So you're going to be one of those silent types, huh?"

"What do you think?" Tommy said.

"I think you're a young man who don't want to spend the rest of your life in jail."

"I don't," Tommy said.

"So start talking."

"Not without a lawyer."

"Okay. Let's take Mr. Dupree back to headquarters," Mark said.

*****

Tommy sat at the table across from Mark, Ken, and a local narcotic cop. They'd allowed him a phone call, so he had called his father. They had agreed to allow his father in the interrogation room, hoping he would convince Tommy that cooperating would be best for him.

J.C. entered the interrogation room, his hair disheveled, and he looked worried.

"What's going on, Tommy?"

"Your son is in deep shit. We've busted him with enough X to supply the whole town," Ken said.

"Son, what happened?"

"The white girl set me up, Dad."

J.C. shook his head. "I can't believe I'm hearing this shit. After we talked, you called her anyway?"

"I did."

"Why did you do this?"

"Dad, I was desperate and I needed the money. Hell, *we* needed the money."

J.C. looked at Mark and Ken. "So you want him to rat?'"

"Not *rat* ... help himself. Cooperate."

"Whatever," J.C. said. "Can I talk to my son alone?"

The door opened and a black female walked in and stared at Tommy.

Tommy smiled. "Alicia! Damn, I'm glad to see you. How'd you know I was here?"

She looked at Tommy for a second then turned her head. She couldn't face him. "Tommy, my name is Stacey Matthews."

"Your name is Alicia."

"Tommy, I work for the DEA, and I was working to infiltrate your crew."

"What are you, some kind of government snitch or something?"

"No, I'm an agent."

"Agent my ass." Tommy laughed.

She showed him a badge.

"Is this some kind of joke or something?"

"I wish it were but it's not."

"What about Don?"

"Actually, the man Don is not an agent; he's a paid informant. He goes around and sets people up for us. He receives twenty-five percent of everything we confiscate. The money you gave him, he'll get a percentage."

"I don't understand," Tommy said.

"Tommy, I was only doing my job."

"Fuck you! Bitch, you ruined my life."

"Tommy, I'm sorry."

"What part of the game is this? You meet a nigga; you fuck a nigga; and then you help send a nigga to jail."

"I don't know what you're talking about; I've never slept with you."

"I can describe your pussy lips. What's the point in lying about it?" Tommy shouted angrily.

Stacey Matthews pointed at him. "He's lying."

"Tommy, we got you. Don't you see? There's nothing you can do. We've got you," Mark said.

"The hell I can't. This shit is entrapment. I'll get me a lawyer and get out of this."

J.C. said, "I need to talk to my son alone."

Mark said, "We're giving you five minutes alone."

J.C. looked at Tommy. "Man, this is serious."

"I know, Dad ... I know."

"I wish you would have just listened to what I said. Hell, you even said that something wasn't right."

"Greed got the best of me."

"They are going to want you to set somebody up."

"I already know this. I can't do that, Dad."

"I know you can't; you're too much like me. But in order for you to get out again, you're going to have to at least start to help them. In the meantime, I'll talk to my attorney. If you really slept with this agent, there must be something we can do about this shit. This has to be entrapment or something."

Tommy looked at J.C. with serious eyes. "Dad, that bitch was certainly my girlfriend."

Mark and Ken walked back in the room. "So what did you decide?"

"He's going to help you," J.C. said.

Ken smiled. "No, he's going to help himself."

"Whatever."

"Okay, let's talk about Manny Gomez and his brother Hector."

"I don't want to talk about them," Tommy said. "I don't know them."

"So you're going to play stupid," Ken said.

"Tommy, your telephone records clearly show that you talked to Manny extensively," Mark said.

"I feel more comfortable starting at the bottom and working my way to the top."

Mark opened a Manilla folder. "What about Joe Ingram?"

"What about him?"

"You think you can get him to make a buy?"

"I'm not going to help you bring down my friend."

"Your friend? This guy was banging your girl."

"What the fuck are you talking about? How did you know this? Did that bitch tell you that?"

"Who are you talking about?" Clark said.

"Agent Matthews."

"Mr. Dupree, we've had all of your phones tapped for several months now," Mark said.

Tommy took a deep breath. "I can't set my friend up. Anybody but Joe."

"Doesn't look like you're starting at the bottom. Maybe we should start you off in a bottom bunk." Mark said.

"Hey, start with Joe," J.C. said.

Tommy looked at his father but didn't say anything.

"Okay. We're going to need him to make a sell to him and wear a wire."

"When?" Tommy asked.

"Now, before he learns that you're in trouble."

"Daddy, I don't want to do this shit."

"Son, it's going to be okay."

Tommy hugged his father.

*****

JoJo knocked on Tommy's door and was invited inside. "What's up, nigga?"

"What's up, Joe?"

Tommy turned the pocket-size recorder on.

"What you got for me?"

"Hold on a second … I'll show you."

Tommy walked toward a backroom. Seconds later, he came back with a bag.

"Let me check everything out."

"Hold on, Joe. Not so fast," Tommy said.

"The money is in the car, I'll go get it, but first I need a bag or something to put it in. The bag I got is plastic, and you can see right through it."

Tommy felt uneasy about the conversation. He was staring at the drugs, but his mind was somewhere else. He was recalling a memorable childhood moment that involved JoJo, a time that was long before Nia had entered the picture.

"What the fuck is wrong with you, nigga, why you acting so strange?"

Tommy put an index finger to his lips.

"I don't understand," Joe said. "What's wrong?"

"Nothing's wrong."

"Okay, I'm going to get it." Joe began backing toward the front door, confused.

Tommy stopped him with a hand gesture then whispered in Joe's ear, "Don't come back. Better me than you. Please don't come back." Tears were in his eyes.

Joe looked at Tommy's face. He understood. He opened his mouth and lip synced, "Thanks."

Tommy left through the back door.

Around the corner, in the parking lot of the Harris Teeter grocery store, J.C. waited in an old Electra 225.

Tommy jumped in the car and reclined the seat.

"You okay, son?"

"I'm good."

"Let's get the hell out of here. Fuck the police. Motherfuckers always wanting us to do their job." J.C. laughed.

"We got to get the hell out of here fast."

"Don't worry; I got this, Son," J.C. said then he sped off. They rode down Trade Street, ironically, past the federal courthouse. A roadblock was ahead—*Men Working*. J.C. turned off Trade then looped around to Third Street. He made his way to S. Tryon St. From there he got onto I-77 southbound. He would go to the Woodlawn exit to Billy Graham Parkway to I-85 to Atlanta. They would hide in Atlanta for a few days then fly to Alaska if Tommy could get his hands on a fake ID.

When they reached Woodlawn Road, an unmarked police car pulled them over. Then a Blazer pulled beside them. The Toyota Tacoma with agents Pratt and Clark pulled in front and blocked them in.

There was nowhere for J.C. to go. "Goddamn stankin ass cops!" J.C. yelled.

CHAPTER 31

Tommy's bond was denied, but J.C. bonded out because his charges weren't as serious. As soon as he bonded out he contacted Charles S. Finley, Esq. Finley was representing J.C. on his lawsuit against the state for false imprisonment. J.C. was interested in getting representation for his son on a criminal charge. Finley only handled civil suites but referred J.C. to another lawyer in the firm, Dan Huntley, a former federal prosecutor. "Dan is one helluva defense attorney. But let me warn you, he cost a pretty penny. He's worth it; he gets respect in that courthouse."

"How much do you think he would charge?"

"If I had to guess, I would say fifty to a hundred thousand bucks, depending on the case."

J.C. took a deep breath. "Man, you know I don't have that kind of money; I just got out of prison, remember?"

"I wish I could do something to help you, Mr. Cannon."

"Why don't you advance me some of the lawsuit money? Come on, you know we're going to win this case. Hell, they locked me up for nothing. This is an open and shut case; you know this. They already offered me three-hundred thousand dollars, so you know I'll have enough to pay this Huntley guy."

"I tell you what, I'll talk it over with Dan. I'll see if we can work something out."

"Promise."

"Yeah, I promise."

"If you two can work something out, I will double Huntley's legal fees after I get my settlement."

"You really love your son, don't you?"

"He's all I got in this world."

"Mr. Cannon, don't worry about it. I will make it happen."

"Thanks."

*****

Dan Huntley was a tall redhead with a freckled face. He wore huge glasses. A no-nonsense kind of guy, he was an ex-military man. He'd also worked hard as a federal prosecutor for ten years, bringing down some of the city's most notorious criminals. He decided to go into private practice when one of his old law school buddies started his own firm. He was offered a partner position. He'd become quite wealthy since becoming a criminal defense attorney. He'd bought himself a penthouse and a Ferrari, and he'd invested in eighteen condos that he used as rental properties. His net worth had tripled.

Huntley extended his hand to Tommy when he walked into the attorney visitation room in the county jail.

"Pleased to meet you, sir," Tommy said.

"How ya feeling, big guy?"

"Not so good."

"I can understand that, but I'm going to do my best to get you out of this situation—or at least put you in a better position."

"I hope so."

"Your dad said something about you being sexually involved with one of the agents involved in the case."

Tommy's eyes lit up. "Yeah, one of agents was a woman."

"What was her name?"

"Stacey Matthews. She went by the name of Alicia."

Huntley scribbled the names on a yellow legal pad. "And you and Matthews were supposedly an item, huh?"

"Yeah."

"They must have thought you were a big fish."

"Why do you say this?"

"This is a pretty intense investigation."

"You think so?"

Huntley nodded. "The way they lured you into investing your money with the CI and all … that was serious."

"Is that entrapment?"

"Yes and no. It's kind of dirty the way they can persuade you to do something like invest your money while pretending to be your friend, but they can do it within their bounds. Entrapment is hard to prove."

"Sleeping with the target of an investigation isn't illegal?" Tommy asked.

Huntley took his glasses off. "This is clearly government misconduct, but how are you going to prove it? It's going to be her word against yours."

"I don't know?"

"That's what I was afraid of. You have no proof. We'll have to try this from another angle, unless we can prove your allegation. Let's face it, I don't think she's going to come forward and say that she slept with you."

"But we used to be together everyday; my friends used to see us."

Huntley stared at Tommy without smiling. "Son, I believe you, but the judge probably won't. I'm just being realistic."

*****

"So how does it look?" J.C. asked Tommy, staring through the Plexiglass window.

"I guess it's okay. Huntley says we can't get an entrapment defense."

"Why?"

Tommy shrugged. "Says the judge rarely rules entrapment."

"Even if you sleep with the feds."

"I guess."

"That's fucked up, Son."

"I know it is."

"You say your prayers?"

"I did."

"Well then keep your head up; everything is going to be okay."

Tommy ran his fingers through his hair. "You know we only get one haircut a month in here."

J.C. chuckled. "Is that why your ass is looking like the missing link between man and ape?"

"Very funny. I remember coming to see your ass in here, and you was looking like Dr. J. from back in the day."

J.C.'s smiled disappeared. "Son, I hate they got you caged like an animal."

"Don't worry, Dad. Like you say, everything is going to be okay."

"It will; I really believe that," J.C. said.

"Me too."

"I hate that DEA bitch, and I don't even know her."

"I just feel so fucking used. I loved this woman; I really did. I actually had a lot of fun with the woman."

"I know she's a nasty 'lil bitch."

"Why you say that?"

"I found a pair of bloody underwear in your apartment. They were thongs. And I know they couldn't have been yours, or at least I hope not."

"Naw, they weren't mine, player."

"I hope not."

Tommy's eyes lit up. "Those underwear, that's the proof I need."

"What you talking about?"

"My semen is on those underwear, too. I pulled those thongs to the side to hit that, but I remember coming out sloppy."

J.C. smiled. "Tommy, this is good news, Son. That means your DNA and her DNA is on them. The same thing that got me out of prison is going to get you out, too."

*****

"Did you have sex with him?" Mark asked Stacey.

"No."

"His lawyer is claiming that you did, and he has proof."

"Well, I didn't. What kind of proof?"

"He won't tell us, but he says that he's going to make our whole department look corrupt."

"Fuck what he says; I know what I done," Stacey said. She sipped some coffee.

"Again, did you fuck the man?"

"Did you fuck the white girl?"

"This ain't about me?"

"The hell it ain't; it's about the department."

"Hey, I just don't want anybody to get embarrassed, that's all."

Stacey began to cry.

Mark looked down at her. "It's going to be all right."

"I'm sorry. I swear I'm sorry."

Mark ran his fingers through her hair then whispered, "We all make mistakes." He thought about the sex he'd had with Jennifer, but she

226

had taken the secret to the grave with her.

Stacey raised her head, looked into his eyes for a moment, then started crying again.

*****

"Good news," Huntley said.

Tommy smiled. "What is it?"

"The girl resigned from the agency."

"Oh yeah? What does this mean?"

"In my opinion it means that she isn't going to dispute the allegations."

"So what does this mean for me?"

"Nothing. You'll probably be debriefed by outside agents about your affairs." Huntley toyed with an ink pen. "Tommy, you're facing a minimum twenty years. I'm going to ask the judge to give you a reduction since you came forth with the information about the governmental misconduct."

"Can you get it down to ten years?"

"Possibly lower."

Tommy smiled. He felt blessed. He extended his hand to Huntley. "You're the best."

"I told you I would put up a fight, and it still ain't over."

"But at least one day I'll be able to live again."

"Yes, indeed you will." Huntley smiled then left the room.

*****

Judge Theodore Owens looked over his glasses at Tommy. J.C. held his son's hand.

Tommy's whole body shook.

"Son, I want you to know that you've done an admirable thing by coming forth with this information. I commend you for helping bring this kind of government corruption to the forefront."

Tommy smiled.

Owen's face became stern. "You are nobody's angel, though. In fact, you've done a lot of harm to the community. Do you understand me?"

"Yeah-yes, sir," Tommy said.

"Your lawyer thinks you should have a second chance."

Huntley raised his hand. "Your Honor, if I may say something?"

"Make it quick."

"Tommy's father is here today. Let me just say he has just completed ten years in state prison."

"So he takes after his father, huh?" Owens said.

"Not quite Your Honor, you see, Mr. Connors was falsely accused and recently released because of new evidence."

"Okay, what does that have to do with this case?"

"Mr. Connors has filed a lawsuit against the state and will probably be awarded a hefty amount of money."

"I don't understand."

"He plans to open a restaurant and several other businesses, so whenever his son released, he will have something legitimate to do. I don't think we'll ever have to worry about him selling drugs again."

"Is this so, Mr. Dupree?"

"Yes, sir, Your Honor."

The prosecutor protested and made a few objections, which were all overruled.

"All things considered, I herby sentence you to sixty months."

"Thank you, Your Honor."

"Thank God!" J.C. said.

EPILOGUE

J.C. was in his new boat, lying back, taking in the sun. His boat was a decent size, but he was thinking of getting something a little bigger, perhaps a river yacht. He could afford it; he could afford a lot of things now that he'd received his settlement for false imprisonment. With the money came new relatives and young women that wouldn't have ordinarily given him a second look, but ever since they had published his settlement in the newspaper, he'd become one of the most popular bachelors in town. He didn't care about women or a new boat; all he wanted in life was to be living when his son walked out of that federal prison. Thirty more months and Tommy would be free. Together they would explore the world, ride in big boats, go deep sea fishing. J.C. smiled, thinking about what life would be like once his boy was free.

ABOUT THE AUTHOR

K. Elliott resides in Charlotte, North Carolina. Elliott participated in and has completed various creative writing courses at both Central Piedmont Community College and Queens University. In 2001, Elliott received a scholarship to attend the North Carolina Writer's Network Conference. Elliott was also a finalist in 2001 Keystone poetry competition. The release of his first novel, Entangled, placed Elliott on the list of Essence best-selling authors. He has also recently signed to write for the G-unit book series.

Other titles available from
Urban Lifestyle Press...

30% OFF

Regular $15.00

Now On Sale! $10.50
Only valid with coupon.

30% OFF

Regular $15.00

Now On Sale! $10.50
Only valid with coupon.

To order online visit
www.beststreetfiction.com

Male orders please send cashiers check or money order to:
P.O. Box 12714 • Charlotte, NC 28220

Other titles available from
Urban Lifestyle Press...

Name: _____

Address: _____

City/State: _____

Zip: _____

	TITLES	PRICES
	Entangled	$13.95
	Fetish	$14.95
	Tennis Shoe Pimp	$15.00
	In The Cut	$15.00

FREE SHIPPING

TOTAL $_____

To order online visit
www.beststreetfiction.com

Male orders please send cashiers check or money order to:

P.O. Box 12714 • Charlotte, NC 28220